THE CASTING COUCHERS

by

I0525960

CHARLES NUETZEL

WRITING AS "STU RIVERS"

The Borgo Press
An Imprint of Wildside Press

MMVII

Copyright © 1961, 2007 by Charles Nuetzel
Originally published under the pseudonym, Stu Rivers.

All rights reserved.
No part of this book may be reproduced in any form
without the expressed written consent
of the author and publisher.
Printed in the United States of America

SECOND EDITION

CONTENTS

INTRODUCTION

Well, I had my personal introduction to show business on several levels. But we won't reflect on that—this isn't true confessions time—yet! I'll simply say that my father was a commercial artist who worked for a company that made the title (screen credits) for most major motion pictures at the time (the early 1940s and '50s). If you look carefully, it is still possible to find "Pacific Title" in the credits of some new flicks. I did my time at one of these small firms (Studio Film Service), working as a cameraman and discovering the complexities of the sound stage and set and other related items. As for the biz itself, well, I even worked a short stint there. But that's another story.

When I wrote *Whodunit? Hollywood Style*, the book that became *Hollywood Mysteries* (also published by Wildside Press), it gave me some background information on the history of life behind the scenes and behind the stages of the movie-making capital of the world. I later expanded on this by penning a series of novels with Hollywood and motion-picture production settings, and also by doing further research on the business and its usual practices.

I now know quite a bit more about the world in general and Hollywood in particular then I did forty years ago. Among other things, I was given a kind of guided tour into the life of the performer by a real-life professional singer, who has a minor walk-on in the present version of this novel. Its new theme derives partially from some of the background data and anecdotes she supplied.

The Casting Couchers was originally published under the pseudonym of Stu Rivers, which I employed fairly frequently in my early days as a writer, together with his companions, John Davidson, George Fredrics, and Fred Mac-Donald, among many others. Maybe someday I'll write a piece about the joy of being a pen name.

—Charles Nuetzel
Thousand Oaks, California
July 2006

CHAPTER→①

There were two problems running through Peter Denton's mind as he drove his blue sedan toward the *Van Horn Studios.* The strongest, at that moment, was the delightful memory of a warm and sweet-tasting kiss from Judy Grant, whom he had been forced to leave alone at his apartment.

A call from the studio had brought a warm passionate scene to a quick and awkwardly blunt end.

It was a bad time for any kind of business, but he couldn't have ignored the phone because it might be Mr. Calvin Van Horn. When the "Big Man" said jump, there were a lot of people in Hollywood who would do just that—and willingly! Peter Denton was one of those puppets. And a newly hired one who very much wanted to succeed at his first job as a producer. Everything mattered. Even with a low level Hollywood big shot like Van Horn who had been in the business for decades and knew all the tricks to put out fast films for quick profits.

A real chance for Peter Denton's hopes of making it big in films. He had put aside all thoughts of romantic involvements as childish fantasy; business was business. It came first. Family and all that were something he simply had decided could wait. Even if that had been a lovely dream in early years. Now it was all different. And the unlimited extras of the casting couch were a neat little bonus that came along with the job title.

The phone conversation had been brief but to the point: "Get the hell on down here, Sweetheart! I have a nice big shock waiting for you!"

"What?"

"Alice Palmer again!"

That was all the explanation he had needed. The young blonde actor, who was starring in Calvin Van Horn's newest movie production, had been a headache from the very first moment they'd approached her for the role. She'd been getting worse ever since. At this point things didn't matter too much—production was still several days away. They could afford to pamper her; but once things started moving, everybody was ready for the worst.

The "great" actor would be late for shooting, holding up the production; a lot of false temperament; rewriting of the script to suit her own tastes; and arguments with the director, producer and writer.

That would be par for the course; and Mr. Van Horn had known what he was getting himself into when he'd signed her up. The only reason he had done it was because of her big box office drawing power; and that was always very important in the business of making pictures. Star power! And that meant an easy bankroll.

Now whatever was bugging her had to be explosive enough to get the "Big Man" upset:

That was enough for Denton.

He had worked for the man from time to time, free-lancing, but nothing as important as dealing with this picture. Everybody knew Van Horn. Everybody had worked for him indirectly or right under his brutalizing, dictatorial thumb. He was a standard joke and a standard stepping stone for countless now quite famous actors, directors, writers, and producers. It seemed as if the Horn had blown down the throats of most professionals. He was basic training for many hard working people who had been ground through his carnival of hack productions.

Many beginners and even solid freelance personnel bowed to the sound of his trumpeting call, morning, noon or midnight. At least those who wanted a good start or simply a quickie job! It was a mixed bag of wannabees and has-beens who flocked to his side, right along with some very serious long time professionals.

Still, the call to the studio had come at a bad time. It

was one of those long week-ends and Van Horn had given him a couple of days off, because of the hard grind that would follow once production really got started. So, he'd taken the chance to shack-up with his girl of the moment, *Judy Grant,* an attractive young red-headed starlet, trying to get her first big break in the pictures. She'd been around Hollywood all her life and now was hard pressing for a serious acting career.

He was doing what he could to get her a part in the up-coming movie. So far all he had promised Judy was that he'd talk to Van Horn about her. It would always be easy to write in a part for her even at the last moment.

Things between Denton and Judy had started out as usual: young starlet out to make the right connection. Victor Bolton, the writer of the Alice Palmer script, had introduced them a few months ago, and Denton had instantly been interested. She was a charming, sexy young lady. At first it was a matter of "why not" if the woman was willing to enjoy the casting couch game. But it didn't take long before he had become truly interested in really helping her.

At the time of the phone call they had been in the shower, stripped to the raw, enjoying the delightful pleasure of washing one another. The texture of her flesh had always been inviting, but when soapy and wet it was quite exciting.

As his hands brushed her breasts, soaping them until even their rosy centers were hidden under the white suds, he heard her deep sigh of pleasure, and she moved close, running her lips against his neck, nibbling and moaning.

"You feel so good!" she sighed, crushing herself tightly against him. Her hips thrust hard and anxiously against his and he felt the gentle claw of her nails on his back.

He let his hands explore every curve and swell, and then after a long moment their lips crushed together. She was a wonder and actually moaned if soft joy when the kiss broke.

"Now..." she whispered very softly.

He shook his head, smiling, pulled her from the shower and started to dry her. Every caress of the towel on her skin caused a joyous sigh to tremble from her lips.

It was only a matter of seconds before the two of them were stretched out on his large double bed locking their bodies in a tight passionate embrace.

That's when the cell phone rang on the bed stand.

"Don't!" she pleaded, teasing against him in a manner designed to keep him in place.

"Have to!" he simply said, gently taking her hand when it reached down between them in eager search. "No."

"I thought you liked that!" she giggled.

"Do. But…if that's the Big Man I have no choice. You know that. It's my studio cell phone! Business before pleasure."

"I'm at least pleasure!" she smiled happily.

"It demands instant attention! Dear lady."

"And I don't?" she complained, brightly as he picked up the small cell.

He got off the bed, went into the hallway. Once the conversation was over, he returned to Judy who was anxiously waiting. Her full dominant breasts stood invitingly upright pressed together between her hands.

"They're waiting!" she giggled. "All ready and for your…" She saw the look on his face. "You have to go?"

"I'd like to tell Van Horn to go blow his cork!"

They both laugh at that because the man was famous for using that line any time he got angrily.

So it had been a quick goodbye kiss instead of the complete works they both had wanted. One thing he could say about Judy was she enjoyed him—almost as much as he was delighted with her. They had fun together.

"You won't be gone long, will you?" she had signed, disappointment wrinkling her creamy forehead.

"Back as soon as possible," he'd promised.

* * * * * * *

Shaking his head in order to clear that pleasant memory, Denton directed his car off the Hollywood freeway cutoff and down Vine Street. A few minutes later he brought it to a stop in the private parking lot of the *Van Horn Studios*.

Then he was walking into the private chambers of the

Big Man.

And here stood his future, and the future of every one in his employee. The Master Horn blower in his inner chambers. Pictures of famous celebrities lined the walls, most with the Big Man hugging, kissing or shaking hands with the named star. Several posters were framed, announcing the release of one hit picture of another from Van Horn Productions.

"Well, it took you one hell of a damn time to get here, Sweetheart!" the tall thin nervous man exclaimed. As usual there would be no socially polite interchange. It was right to the point, without any nonsense.

"What's the bit?" Denton asked, sitting opposite the powerful white-haired executive-producer.

"Trouble, nothing but trouble, Sweetheart. This darling slut we got as a star is blowing her cork!"

"What now?"

"It seems she got a threatening letter. You know the kind. Crank. A nut of some kind is saying she won't live to play the role in our movie! Oddly enough, she hasn't made it public...yet. Interesting that. But she called us about it. Me. At home! Mind you!" He tossed his hands in the air. "Cries like a whimpering banshee! 'Help me help me, daddy mine!' was her plea over my, personal, private cell. Well words like that! I'm not her daddy!"

"Thank God for sweet blessings," Denton suggested with a weak smile.

"Blessings to hell! I don't like this, Pete! Crank or not. Smells like shit, looks shitty, so must be a bunch of you know what..."

The note was no doubt crank, but that wouldn't matter to Alice Palmer. The woman would blow the whole thing way out of proportion. The police would be called in. The media. By the time she got through it would be headlined on cable channels screaming how Alice Palmer had been almost shot to death. Maybe even the suggestion of having been sexually assaulted. That kind of juicy bit would certainly feed into her own self-image as a woman for which men uncontrollably lusted. She'd throw in a lot of other things, given the chance. The woman was a master at playing the media for all it was worth.

Yet, strangely enough, she hadn't already connected with her media pals.

That suggested just something different.

But anything serious couldn't be kept silent.

"She'll make a big deal out of this one...I take it you sent somebody over to her place?"

"Sure, sure, Sweetheart. Think I was born yesterday? Hell, yes! Damned right! Got Eugene Bass over there handling police to keep it QT. He had enough connections there, and IOUs and all that...and I told him to be free with a few bills if necessary. He knows his business. A subtle, deceptive man, he is. Appears shy and easy going, but he's sly and sharp witted and knows his business. And that's why he's part of the team!"

Denton sighed in relief. "He'll take care of it, all right!"

"I would hope so! Well, I mean, the cops and media." The man shrugged. "But...don't be too sure about the rest of it all, Sweetheart! Alice has blown the lid off things in the past and is already starting to toy around with this. Says she's not doing the part now. That's why I called you over. The police and crud media...well, that's for Bass to squash. That's not the problem!"

"What about the contract? She certainly can't..."

"Contract shmontract! Who gives a damn?" Van Horn exploded, standing and walking around his desk. "That's ironclad. But she's got to want to play, willingly. Otherwise we're in a publicity mess. And more! And this *is* the point, mind you, the money can be yanked! Some of our backers weren't too happy having her in the deal—regardless of her draw! She bankable. Sure. And she's danger city! You know what a woman like Alice can do? She can blow hell out of any production. Be late, come drunk, and act on one cylinder. When she does a bad job it *will* cost money. Lots of money! And I'll have to drop her—then she takes us to court on breech of contract. To hell with a contract! If she doesn't want to do the part, she has our balls in her crusher! Right over a barrel in two ways. We need her for the role. She's perfect! It was made for her—written for her! Anyway...

she's good box office! And we've invested too much on this film to have it blown away! The studio had some bad breaks last year. Even with cable and DVDs—you can't sell shit! Even to the public. Well, to me its all crap now days. Just not my choice. Miss the old days when you told a story about people! Small films are hard to sell to the big bankers!" The man shrugged. "Anyway…she's kept it quite for the instant!" He grew silent for a thoughtful moment, then said softly: "Really a puzzle that. All of it!"

"And what do you want me to do?"

"Use your head, Sweetheart! That's what I pay you for. You go over to her place and convince her she's got to play along with us. That she can't get out of the contract and that there is no point of being afraid of a crank letter! In other words: somehow get her to forget the *whole* thing…Keep it smart. Do whatever she demands—as long as she comes out on our side. *I* don't care how you do it. Offer her money. Anything. Say we'll hire some damn private dick for her. Anything. I don't care how you handle it. But handle it! Just do me a favor and get her off my back!"

"When do you want me to see her?"

"Come on, Sweetheart. Go right now! Cut her off short before things really begin to get bad. Prostrate your bod stark naked if necessary. If she says fuck, do it!" That last brought a grim smile on the man's lips. "Actually, she's pretty good at that!"

The man came to a halt in front of Denton. "Look, I want her to be nice. See what I mean? I want her to calm down." His arms flung themselves in the air. "Off my back! See what I mean? That's what I pay you for!"

Denton saw exactly what Van Horn meant. It was simple. He got the Palmer girl off the Big Man's back, or he didn't have a job the next morning. And that meant doing whatever was necessary.

Without another word he turned and walked out of the office. Next stop was Alice Palmer's Beverly Hills home.

CHAPTER→ℓ

Eugene Bass was organizing the media when Denton arrived. A small crowd of media personnel had already set in around her house. Luckily it was only local people. So he offered up the official studio statement on the threatening note, meant to offset anything Miss Palmer might say.

"Where is she?" Denton asked the press agent.

"In there!" Bass answered, pointing toward the double doors which led to the play room.

Alice Palmer looked up as he entered, her face lined from tragic emoting. But every hair was in place, every atom of makeup in flashing sexual perfection. She was onstage; in a role; before imaginary cameras. The tight-fitting, low-cut sweater and flaring skirt accented every famous line of her body. The large breasts which fought up tight against the low-cut neck-line of the sweater were happily displayed. There was a sparkling necklace which looked almost out of place against the creamy whiteness of her throat. The large awkward bracelets were out of place on her arms. But that was Alice Palmer. Flash and sex.

She was a woman that men dreamed about; and, apparently, many had enjoyed. Her rep was almost outlandish. At least that fit her public image.

In the way she had used her body it was impossible to ignore a natural invite to enjoy staring. No man would kick her out of bed. And she knew it.

Alice Palmer was a lush, walking sexual animal. And what was captured on film was a natural manner in the flesh. She studied him in a very calculating way, as if mentally defining the make of this male animal now in her presence. They had had dealings in the office, but never at her home.

14

And her eyes brushed over his frame, boldly assessing what they saw. Her expression became quiet invitation. But she made no obvious move towards him. It was all a natural manner of a woman who enjoys flirtations with attractive men. She made no secret about finding him very promising.

"Now what do you want, Darling?" she demanded in that icy clipped tone of voice that had become her trademark in the films. It was lower than usual; a little heavier with emotion. Melodramatic. She was playing the scene for all it was worth.

She stood and picked up a golden cigarette case. "Want one?"

He declined the offer. She placed a cigarette between her lips, holding it there in an almost caressing manner before lighting it. Her eyes never left his, and the small twinkle of amusement flashed warmly as he watched her.

"These are bad for your health, but I love smoking," she said, after lighting up and taking a very long drag. "Well, I'm quite oral, you know. These help!"

She laughed in delight at his quick response to those words. "Don't let me shock you."

"I'm not!"

She literally stripped him naked with her eyes, as they roam all over him with blatant amusement. "But…well, never mind that, right now."

Then she shifted, became all business, distracted. "We do have other matters!"

"Want to talk about it?" he asked in as soft and soothing a tone as he could manage. First he would have to play the "big brother" act; then, if that didn't do any good, he would have an attempt at reasoning with her. After that it would be threatening, and then last of all, bargaining.

"Didn't the Big White Father Van Horn tell you?" she questioned, blowing smoke in his direction. That was one trick she had learned from one of her past directors and had used in real life ever since. Hiding behind the smoke.

"Of course! What else?" He tried to sound like a fellow conspirator, for he knew she didn't like Calvin Van Horn—not too many people did—and there was always the chance of getting her on his side by playing it her way.

"Don't game me! I'm not in the mood. Draw a bottom line. And we can…bounce it around."

"He's hoping you'll be reasonable about things."

"What things?"

"Said you were frightened by a note."

"Well, it would scare the shit out of you, too. Did you read it?"

"I know about it. He…we…figure it's a crank."

"Crank or not. I'm wanting out! Best to keep my head in place for better things!" She flashed a quick glance at his lean frame. "Movies aren't life."

"That's not what I've heard!" he countered, jokingly. "Come on, don't take it all so seriously."

"I'll take what I like!" she snapped, eyes suddenly very hard as they met his. Then the woman smiled, wide, exposing lovely white teeth. "I always take what I like! All the better to know you!"

That was so abrupt that Denton blinked in surprise.

She laughed, throatily, "We really must become friends…of course. But—this is business."

It was difficult to keep from responding, but he held down any verbal comment. His body was on automatic stage one lust. If she said jump, he would not be able to avoid jumping quite high to take her on. The very idea made him somewhat heady.

She knew exactly what he was feeling and leaned back in contented amusement, watching, saying nothing, just letting him drink in her sensuously posed body. She was being the star, the queen, enjoying his obvious discomfort. The woman was playing him like a damned fool kid in heat.

Almost angrily he said: "Well, first of all we have a contract and we expect it to honor to the fullest! A two-way street. That's what he wanted me to tell you."

She shrugged as if not caring and said: "You can tell him to take his contract and shove it up...his nose!"

He managed a forced laugh at that, then said: "Well, Miss Palmer—he wants to do anything to help."

"Call me Alice, or something more friendly!" she insisted.

16

"Okay. Alice." Using that first name was almost like a caress in his throat. He gulped on the word. Then continued: "He's willing to get investigators to look into it, if you want. Body guards to make you feel safe."

"I have all the body guards I need. I can call my own PI to investigate!" she snapped back. "But, quite frankly, the way things are nowadays, with car bombers, terrorist, crazy people all over…I don't know."

"Give the guy a break. Let the studio handle this. We don't want it to become a media show! That's all we need."

"Any publicity is good publicity. Don't you think?" she offered, lighting another cigarette.

"Not so," he assured her.

"Don't try to screw me around!" she blurted, then reconsidered. "Well, not right here and now, that is!"

The woman laughed at that and the startled look on his face. "I *do* shock you?"

"No. Just your switch …" He fumbled mentally, then added: "You tend to…"

"Oh, stop. My mind is too fast for most people. I guess I take some getting used to, Sweetie. I hope you'll get used to me, all of me, really, over time." She blew smoke between them, murmured almost to herself: "that might be nice, really nice."

Then her eyes became hard. "Van likes to blow his Horn, as well as his…well, cork? I don't want his damn studio wine gagging my act!"

"He wants to control the media show, if it comes to that. Let him. Better that way."

"Blow your nose, kiddo!" she sneered, so nastily that it was like a physical blow across the face. "He's a control freak! Don't suck his…cork! He'll blow you away. And I don't like the message you're giving me!"

"You know I'm just doing a job."

"Sure…but, I'm not!"

"Look, I'm just a messenger boy."

"Okay, Darling," she sighed, tired, abruptly changing her mood to that of a person forced to be indulgent to a small ignorant child. "What does Father Horn want this time? Tell me and get it over with. Messenger boy!" She sighed, shrugged. "Okay…just drop it on the floor so I can stomp all over it!"

Denton found it hard to keep his eyes away from the dip at the top her sweater. She couldn't help noticing, but did nothing about it.

"I understand you said something about walking out on the picture."

"So?"

"You can't do that!"

"That's old news. Don't bore me. Bottom line is, that note is scary stuff, and the movie is shit, quite frankly. I don't need dumb lines to read out. I want changes made. I can't let my career falter on dumb writing, dumb scripts, dumb films, dumb, dumb, dumb!"

So that was the bottom line. And what else did she want, he wondered.

"Calm down a little. Don't get so excited. Things like that are small issues. Easily ironed out."

"Easy for you to say. But a girl has to hold on to her reputation, you know," she said in a swift change. "I'm a lady who has to make her living on that reputation. I have a high style life. And I enjoy it. And all the lovely benefits that fall in line…eager to lap up the crumbs I might drop their way. Men are so basically deliciously simple-minded—and I simply enjoy the basic things in life. But they can be costly!"

"Then let the professionals deal with all this," was his quick retort.

"And I'm not a pro?" she muttered. Sitting up, breasts thrust out and she brazenly cupped them in her hands. "I'm all that and more, honey. And these honeys are top drawer investments, highly insured cause they're what draws a lot of attention and money at the box office. I'm not dumb. I know where my power is—right here in my hands. Plus all the rest of me. And I demand full cooperation from every-body. Including you and including Mr. Van of the Horn—blow his cork if you will. And that's my message to the Big Man. You can deliver that to him."

Her shifting moods and messages were amazing in both their swift delivery and variety. One moment she was angrily demanding and the next somewhat more flirtatiously playful, cold business, then sultry seductress. It was almost as if the woman couldn't make up her mind what message she wanted to sell him, what mood she wanted to create, what game she actually wanted to play out.

"Why not cooperate with us?" he suggested, soothingly. "We can all work together, surely."

"I would hope so," she murmured, eyes suddenly smoldering. It was almost comical how she shifted to the blatant erotic. She could read an innocent sounding line in an angry, business like way or make it almost a shared orgasm.

"So," she continued, bitingly, "I don't want to be killed! Maybe he'll share that with me?"

"You know that won't happen. You're quite safe. Some nut the authorities will lock up. Don't be melodramatic!"

"I'll be what I damn please!" she suddenly stood, and screamed at him. "And I'm not being 'melodramatic'!" Her voice then softened a little. "And I'm dropping out of this picture. And that's final!"

"I thought we'd agreed. You can't do that!"

"Oh, but Darling, that is exactly what I am doing! I didn't want the part in the first place."

She shrugged. Her breasts played against the cloth stretched against them. She wasn't wearing a bra and the sight was stunning as she stood there gazing at him.

"The contract, remember?" He felt they were going around in circles which she skillfully directed. And he was aware of a sudden shift of mood that seemed to reach out and silently embrace him. It was literally physical, as if the air itself had become electric. The woman knew exactly how to play a scene like this from years of practice on and off the screen. And she was suddenly totally focused.

Without a word she glided towards him, stopping only inches away, looking up into his eyes with soft, liquid desire.

"Oh, those little old contracts can always be broken, can't they?" Her arms slid around his neck, and she pressed close. The feel of her lush body against his was dazzling. "You don't want to cause me any trouble—do you?" Her mouth brushed his and for one brief instant he wanted nothing less than totally ravish her, right there.

"Alice, I wouldn't be so sure of that." The words were thick, voice raspy. He felt like a damned fool.

Her eyes flashed knowingly as she merely moved her hips into his, surging back and forth without any attempt to be subtle. She was playing him on a very basic level and not being in any way coy.

"Delicious," she noted with obvious pleasure at discovering his rapid response. Her mouth, moist and open started lifting to his.

"Do I shock you, now?" she wondered, the words breathing warmly against his lips. Then suddenly, without a pause, she stepped back. "Hate to shock a fella. Not nice of me!"

Her hand brushed over him, touching his chest, then she winked knowingly. "I think you're neat! I could...well, never you mind. Not today!"

She laughed and turned away, totally satisfied at having made her point. If she wanted him as a lover it would take but a touch of her finger tips. "Tell the old man that the contract is paper to use in the...toilet!"

His eyes were fashioned on her back and only with control was he able to step away, rather than grab her and take that wonderful body in his arms.

"You can't dump it. There are lawyers. There are—" he almost shouted.

"There you go again, Darling, with that innocent stuff. Where did you learn all that crap?" She whipped around, facing him. "You know that *I* don't want to do this movie. I never did! All *I* needed *was* an excuse."

"The part's perfect for you! What do you have to lose? Mr. Van Horn *is* paying big bucks..."

"You must be kidding. What contract did he show you?" she demanded with contempt in her voice

"We know he's paying top dollar!"

"So? Is it worth getting killed for?" She walked across, the room. A moment later she returned with a slip of white paper in her hands. "Read this and see what think!"

He read the note. *If you want to continue living, don't do the Van Horn movie!*

20

If he had heard anything that was crank, it was this letter. Straight from cranksville! And was unsigned. Right from a bad movie script.

"You don't take this thing really seriously, do you?"

"Wouldn't you, Darling?"

"No, I'm afraid I wouldn't! Even if I wanted to"

"But, you see, you aren't me. And I *do* take it seriously. And I don't plan on taking *any* chances on my own life. So, out goes the part! The picture! And *everything!* Out walks Miss Alice Palmer!"

She grabbed hold of his arm and moved him toward the door. "I think you should go right on back to 'Big Daddy' and tell him to blow his cork!"

"Hold it!" Denton yelled in a commanding voice, brushing her hand away. "Just take it a bit easy. I'm not through yet!"

"I believe that you are!" she announced. *"I'm finished with you!"*

"Look! Mr. Van Horn said to tell you the contract stays! But he'll hire detectives. Protection. Anything you want!"

Alice Palmer stared at him for a long time: her expression almost showed interest. "We went though that part. Skip to the next scene, please! What else did the 'White Father' offer?"

"What do you mean?" Denton felt a tight knot dig through his insides. There was only one more offer to make. "He's even willing to talk over any...well, money arrangements that might be necessary to get you to change your mind."

Her face lit up like a neon sign advertising one of her own movies.

"Oh, my, surprise, surprise. I was wondering when you'd back off on that hard line. He'll pay more? A percentage! Give me more control over the script. Get me a better custom designer. I want a different director...the list goes on. That's just for starters!" Then she became very serious. "I'll think it over."

She then indicated the door with her eyes. "I think you had better leave now."

Denton was more than glad to get out of there. Now he could return to his apartment and the delightful arms of Judy Grant. In less than twenty minutes he arrived. She was there anxiously waiting, holding a cocktail in her hands, when greeting him. She wore nothing other than his white robe wrapped tightly about her body. He eagerly pulled her into his arms, thrilling to the feel of her, washing away the memory of Alice Palmer in that one lovely embrace.

"WOW!" she exclaimed, hugging to him. "That was worth waiting for!"

He tugged the top of the robe open. She surged against his fingers, eyes closing momentarily.

"That's nice," she murmured. "You're so nice to me!"

That really touched him in a special way. He almost felt guilty about his first impression of Judy as being nothing but a casting couch quickie. Of course that was weeks ago. Things had changed quite rapidly. She was a nice person; he really liked her.

"You're nice to me, Judy."

"Oh, now you're going to give me that ol' Cary Grant 'Judy, Judy, Judy' line?" she giggled.

"The man never said that. Just comics on stage doing him."

She laughed. "You're so serious."

"No I'm not! Just tired! Van Horn plus Alice Palmer can be a double trouble gig destined to drain a man!"

"What's she like?" Judy wanted to know, sipping the drink. "As hot as the media say she is?"

He shrugged. "I suppose."

"Seriously. Is she anything like in the films?" she wanted to know. "Throwing herself into every man's arms?"

"Something like that."

"Does she really devour her men alive?" She offered him her cocktail. "Or is it all just publicity, magic mirrors in the night?"

He blinked down at her. "The woman is a drain on the brain."

"And, I suppose on your dear wonderful bod!" She teased him with a hug. "Did she drain you like some monster

22

creature from outer space? Like she did in her horror flick last year?"

"Hardly."

"Hmmm…I hope that isn't a code word!" she giggled in delight. "Just love the 'H' word! So…firm and fully-packed! Better than a cigarette. More like a lovely, wonderful cigar, don't you think?"

"I couldn't wait to get back to you!" he admitted, sipping the martini.

"Then you aren't too tried?" She teased him with a bright smile.

"No way!" he grinned in relief to be off the subject of Alice Palmer. "All I want now is little old you in my arms. Get Van Horn and Co out of my mind! Enough is enough!"

She suddenly frowned, pulled away, said: "Oh, he called. You'd left your cell here! He was furious!"

It was like a low blow, and a cold chill iced through him.

"What'd he want? Did he say?"

"I guess…he blew his famous cork!'" She laughed at that, then more seriously stated: "He got another call from that Palmer woman just a little while ago," Judy told him, half smiling. "She called him right after you left…and he's burning mad!"

CHAPTER→

That same evening the story hit cable news in a surprisingly small way, merely a comment in the special show-biz shows. But enough to let the world know the bare basics.

Most people hearing the story perked up their ears for a moment and then forgot the matter as other stories flashed rapidly by. The Van Horn PR squad had down played everything.

But Connie Remington missed even that, for she had other more pressing matters centering her attention.

The young woman paced back and forth in her apartment living room, nervous, anxious. This was the night things would happen to change her life.

This night was going to be a turning point. She would be dating a man who might offer a real break—at least she was determined to make the most of it—and not muff it all, like she had so many times before over the past months. Everybody who wanted to break into films had to face this decision one way or another.

Play the casting couch game or simply find a lover with the right connections and pull.

She had come to Hollywood for only one purpose. That was to make a big splash in the movies. Become a Big Star. That was important to her. And at first she hadn't known just how hard it was going to be. After all, if you had talent, it seemed to her, then all you had to do was present it to the right people and on you went to fame. It wasn't that easy, she had quickly discovered in the first few months she'd been in the big town.

Casting directors just weren't interested in young girls with talent and no experience. Maybe casting directors didn't think much of her acting talent because she hadn't had any "credits" in movies or TV. What experience marked her acting history was valid enough and critically acceptable. Home town plays. Amateur shows. But local critics had raved. And her instructors had considered her to be exceptionally talented. A couple of small parts in regional theater had supported their encouragement. All she needed was a break. A chance to apply all that she knew on a professional level.

Nobody in Hollywood had been impressed.

They *were* interested in young girls with little talent and a lot of experience—in bed. But she hadn't been about to use sex as a means to open the doors. At least, not at first.

Not that she was a virgin. Nor cold.

Connie had had her share of lovers; and felt good about them!

So far she'd avoided the casting couch game so many of her friends ended up submitting to. Maybe foolishly. Tonight she might find a middle ground.

What Judy Grant had told her one day in acting class had been almost inspiring: "If you want to get along, you have to play along. Find yourself a good guy! If you're lucky, that'll make all the difference! Believe me! I'm lucky with Pete! He's super nice. And big at Van Horn Studios." The young woman was like an eager child with a wonderful new dress in her hands. It was obvious that she was very much taken by this man—and didn't mind admitting to it. "Even if he never comes up with a part...maybe I'm sorta in love—don't know. Well, in a way, I suppose. Probably just fun and games. But what fun. What games! Yes. I'm sorta crazy about him! But I'm not a fool! I'd be a fool to expect more than we have right now."

Even if Connie knew that Judy was far more involved with the man than she was willing to admit, it was obviously a meaningful relationship between two people enjoying one another. And what was wrong with that? Plus he was willing to help her career, so Judy had stated over and over again.

They had been friends since Connie had met her at the private acting classes they both attended in Burbank. And for a while actually shared an apartment together.

And some weeks ago Judy had introduced Connie to the man taking her out tonight.

She looked at herself in the mirror, enjoying the way the dress hugged her slim body.

Well, if he wanted her, why not? He was connected. And rather nice, in a way.

Why not enjoy a bit of honest feelings with a man? It doesn't have to be conditional. Just a matter of picking the right guy with the right connections and open hearted enough to help her career. And that he was!

Everybody was cramming for a chance at success. And she had to be realistic, she had rationalized all day.

Right now things were changing in her life.

The few weeks ago at one of those Hollywood blow-outs Judy had introduced her to the man. He had made a gentle pass and asked her out. She had been sipping a whiskey on the rocks when Judy came bobbing up.

"Hi there Con!" Judy had cried, motioning a man who was following her, "Here's a guy I want you to meet!"

It was that quick.

"This is Connie Remington—Eugene Bass! See you later!" And a couple of seconds after that the two of them were alone.

"Judy's been telling me about you," Bass said awkwardly.

"I imagine. Probably foolish lies. Hollywood lies. Rumors, flying all around the room. In the streets. All over town about Connie, the struggling young actor getting nowhere fast! So she dumped me on you. So sorry about that!"

Why'd she say that? Normally she wasn't so flip.

Bass laughed. "Guess so. I don't think she wanted to be stuck with me. Or just wanted to play the field—or play Pete—so she dumped me off on you! Lucky me!"

"Nice of you to say, but really, not fair to you!"

"Hey, you're a sport."

"Oh. How flattering," she smiled a bit uncertain. "The sporty type? Yuck!"

"Don't knock yourself! No, you're a real looker."

"Aren't we all?" she inquired. "A lot of fake boobs in this room, along with many altered hips and thighs, nose

26

jobs, chin lobs, lip jobs and …"

"And you haven't had one! That's my bet!" He studied her seriously, offered: "Say you're really lovely! In a nice innocent way."

"I assume that's a compliment. As opposed to in an experience way…"

"Or cheap way? Hardly that!" he offered. "You have class. And that's better"

"Now you're embarrassing me," she admitted, trying to hide the flush on her cheeks.

"No. Quite the opposite. I'm lucky to get to know you! She did me a great favor! Nice to meet somebody…well, nice! I'm just a lonely ol' guy who can't get himself…companionship with out help!"

"Don't say that!" Connie felt suddenly sorry for the man. He seemed to be quite nice, a little unassuming, but nice enough.

They had talked a little while, walked out into the garden, and in the dimness, standing quite close to her, he had reached out and pulled Connie to him. For a moment she hesitated, and then the combination of the drinks and her loneliness and frustration caused her to relax into the embrace,

It didn't last long, but it was long enough. Afterwards he looked at her and then down at his hands. "Sorry—"

"Why?"

"Well you just aren't—I…"

"Forget it!" she told him, then added: "I thought it was rather nice."

They talked for a little while, and she learned that he was a press agent for a small Hollywood producer. Beyond that she learned very little about his personal life.

Some people had joined them before anything actually developed, and there wasn't any time during the rest of the evening to really get to know each other better. Before she had left he'd suggested that they get together sometime soon. They exchanged numbers and parted. She really didn't expect to hear from the man.

A few days ago he'd called her cell phone.

And now tonight was to be their first date. If it meant

intimacy she figured that might be okay. He could, perhaps, help her failing career. If sex turned out to be part of the deal, maybe it wouldn't be so horrible with him. Months of lost chances proved that a change in attitude was needed.

Hollywood could be a city of savage takers. Nobody cared about you, they were too involved in their own needs, own egos, own desperate clawing up the celluloid ladder. And if you didn't play the game by the rules of survival you didn't get up the next frame of film to stardom. In fact, her experience had proven, so far, you couldn't even get into the agent's or producer's or casting director's office. Hell, you couldn't even get to the secretary. For people like her it was reception desk dead end.

Still, playing the casting couch game rubbed her wrong. And she would never give into it as a casual every day routine. In fact, she certainly didn't plan on throwing herself into any man's arms just on a chanced vague promise. Even then, the idea of loose sex for a part simply turned her stomach.

Yet if she wanted to win the game she had to learn to play by the rules, as Judy had advised.

Maybe to many people "starlet" meant cheap easy lay, but it also meant a few small parts in movies or TV as payoffs for a tumble on the couch. From there, so the story went, it was just a matter of continuing from one couch to another until reaching the top!

Or hitting the bottom as a cheap prostitute named "starlet"!

That was one game she was determined to avoid. There had to be a smart way of sleeping your way to the top. The alternative was becoming a lost soul in the shadow of Hollywood sign as all dreams withered. That ended in the nightmare land of prostitution, sleeping in the streets or, perhaps, managing to connect with an escort service. The real lucky ladies became call girls and made thousands of dollars a week, until their bodies were ruined by drugs, Aids or simply worn out by age. That wasn't where Connie planned on heading. No down hill ride into hell.

Nor did she plan on returning home with her tail between her legs and living with the "I told you so" comments of family and friends.

So, maybe, with this guy tonight, she might find a middle, safe ground.

There were thousands like her; talent was cheap. Ambition even cheaper. Everybody wanted in. Few made it. And most of them starved and ended up supporting their "dream habit" with dead end jobs. Too many wannabees and hangers-on populated the film industry world wide.

Connie knew the next hours could change things. If not, then it was back to basics.

Eugene Bass just might be her first breakthrough. The man was rather nice in his way. Certainly not a thrill a minute. But not some crummy little creep behind a large desk who took advantage of desperate young women seeking any part tossed their way.

Carefully she once again arranged the dress around her breasts, which were tightly supported by the bra, to offer a liberal display of flesh. It was one of those form-fitting things that showed that her body had all the curves a man liked to see. And touch. And caress. And...

She muffled those thoughts, embarrassed.

She had always resented the fact that a woman had to make a show of her body in order to get any serious attention. And in Hollywood it was blatant advertisement of assets. Sex was a product that required skillful marketing— even if it was simply: look but don't touch.

Tonight, Connie was ready to step over the that thin line.

The dress pinched at the waist and flared with her hips and thighs, hugging them all the way down to her calves. Her breasts were dutifully offered up as eye-catching trophies for all men to goggle at.

The image in the mirror reflected the message that a man might do more than merely look. It said:

Look *and* touch!

Either way she figured, things would be picking up. At least she'd have a few dates with him. And that'd help in a very practical way. Money was money. Food was high priced. Every free meal was money saved. And she didn't have much of either left. It was get a job as a waitress or typist—or take a chance on the casting coucher's slippery slop to cheap "starletdom."

Just then the door bell rang. She tensed, looked at herself in the mirror. The lipstick was on okay, full and deep red. She moistened her lips with the tip of her tongue. That made her mouth even sexier. The dipping neckline was sure to catch Eugene Bass' eye. The rest of the crimson silk dress hugged her form like an outer layer of shiny skin.

The bell rang once more and she opened the door, smiling and standing in such a way as to accent both her curving hips and bust line.

Eugene Bass just grinned admiringly. "Well now, Beautiful. What can I do for you?"

"Come on in. Want a drink?"

He nodded, leaning closer to enjoy even a closer look down her neckline.

"Aren't you being a bit obvious?" she teased, not moving, letting him just stare. "Naughty naughty!"

"My pleasure, you're dressed to kill! And its killing me!" he chuckled.

"Don't die in my arms, please."

"In you're arms I'd be willing to do anything!"

"Really, now?" she said with pleased amusement, biting her tongue to avoid saying something very *risqué*.

"Well, almost anything. No. Take that back. Rewrite. Paragraph. I'd do anything in your arms. No. Revise. I'd do anything to get you in my arms." He lifted his arms as if to embrace her, but didn't move. Nor did she.

For a moment there was a slight awkward silence, then he said: "What a place you have here!"

But his eyes were fastened on her, moving everywhere at once.

She felt suddenly embarrassed at that open examination. But she didn't look away, merely watched his eyes almost literally caress her. It was, after the first flush, rather pleasing, certainly flattering.

"I had almost forgotten how beautiful and attractive you are."

"Just attractive?" she teased, knowing very well that he was totally taken by what he saw.

30

"Well," he admitted, "you look just grand!"

"Just?" she really laughed at that. "You make me sound like grand piano!"

"Well, quite frankly you have all the class of a magnificent concert grand, if you want to know the truth. You simply took my breath away. You're hardly the lovely lady I met the other day...I mean, merely lovely. I said you had class. And, my dear woman, you have it all over you! Well, more than just class. If you want the truth you're really down right...well...gosh words fail me. Guess I best give you a KISS."

She was startled by that. And he chuckled.

"Keep it Simple Stupid! To me. Not you!"

"KISS? I don't think I've heard that one."

"Well, anyway, you're magnificent in a word...well, 'tain't no better than down right hot—okay, KISS that off to: sexy!"

He looked embarrassed, a bit confused, even flustered in saying that last word. That was so charming that Connie couldn't resist.

She leaned close and brushed his cheeks with her lips.

He almost reached for her, but she glided happily away. "Just a KISS for a KISS! To keep it simple, silly!"

"Nice place you have," he offered, a bit huskily.

"The apartment isn't as great as I'd like. But it'll do until something better is dug up. A girl has to cut corners to get along..."

"A girl like you?" the man's voice choked slightly. "I should think you'd have it made!"

Connie moved across the room, came to a stop before the small kitchenette, where a bottle of whiskey was sitting. "Highball or straight?"

"Anyway you like it!" Bass shrugged, stepping up behind her. "You sure are a something!"

She felt a nervousness flutter through her as his hands circled her waist. They lay there, not moving at first, just taking in the feel of her body.

She fixed the drinks and then turned. He backed away, taking the glass she handed him.

"What do you have planned for this evening?" she inquired, sipping the straight whiskey.

"Well, dancing. Dining. Dancing. Let the evening work out. You ever seen Don Bagley? He's doing a guest gig tonight. There's dancing a little—but he's a swinger!" His hand casually caressed her shoulder, almost as if it was impossible not to touch her. But it was like a man who is totally charmed by a very special, delicate object of art, just slightly frightened of breaking its fragile beauty.

It didn't matter to Connie where they went. It would all be only a part of the act they both had to play; the build-up, so it would look a little nicer when he took her to his apartment, or brought her here or to some hotel room. In a way, she felt a little excited.

Eugene Bass wasn't really such a bad looking guy. Tall. A little balding maybe, but his face was youthful. His body looked hard and muscular. He couldn't be more than thirty-five.

No, she realized thoughtfully taking another sip of her drink, he might not be really all that bad. That thought annoyed her, sent a pang of guilt into place. He was such a nice guy. Rather sweet. Perhaps he would seem different later once they had spent the evening together. Right now he was simply nice, and really not all that exciting.

The drinks finished, he abruptly suggested they leave for dinner.

CHAPTER→➍

A few minutes later they were at an expensive restaurant. The surroundings were dim lights, soft music, and romantic settings. Just the type of place she would have expected to see in some Hollywood movie. They'd never had anything like this in her home town.

He ordered cocktails; a Martini for himself and a Manhattan for her. A few minutes later the drinks arrived. One taste was enough to tell her the cocktails weren't made for children.

"From what I've heard about you," Connie told him, placing the drink in front of her and working the rim with her fingers, "you're something of an important man around town."

"Well, let's say being a press agent sometimes has advantages. But, like today, it can be a headache. You read the papers, see the cable news?"

She shook her head.

"Well, we're having media fun with Miss Palmer."

"Alice Palmer?" she fairly cried, quite interested now. She'd always loved the Alice Palmer moves; in a way it wouldn't be too much to say this star was a sort of idol of hers.

"That little lady can cause more trouble than a pack mad apes—well, that's show biz. I'm sure you aren't interested in it."

"Oh, but I am!" she exclaimed, leaning forward in her eagerness.

"Well...it's all on the news, so common knowledge, now...about a crack letter she got."

"How exciting!"

"Don't kid yourself. There's nothing exciting about it." He told her what the letter had threatened but shrugged it off as nonsense. "Crazy people—do crazy things. Especially in today's world. Just a headache to me and the studio. Miss Palmer plays the threat quite serious!"

"You're kidding!"

"Oh, don't get it all wrong. She knows it's just a crank. The woman isn't stupid. She's only making the most of it. Now she wants a big raise in salary and Mr. Van Horn has blown the roof off. But there's nothing that he can do about it. She has him where the meat eats the flesh! Bad scene!"

"How exciting!" And to her it did sound exciting, especially considering how frustrating her own life had become, focused down to the beginnings of a career that got nowhere fast. Getting the inside look at what happened at the higher levels was fascinating. "Tell me more!"

Bass just smiled at her. He had a boyish quality about him which Connie was beginning to like. He actually wasn't such a bad sort at all.

"Enough of studio gossip. Why don't you tell me something about yourself," he suggested, finishing his drink.

"Oh, really, there's nothing to tell."

"You'd be surprised how much a person can learn about another, simply by what they say about themselves. Or don't say. Sometimes that's even more revealing!"

"Now that sounds down right frightening, Gene."

"How's that?"

"Well, you have me up against a rock and a hard place. If I tell all I'm exposed. If I tell nothing I'm…exposed in unknown, unlimited ways that may or may not be the truth. You have me trapped!"

"Check mated, anyway."

"Well let's leave it at checked!" she offered with a quick smile.

"Okay. Checked. So, give me a peek at the real Connie." His eyes instinctively caressed over her as if imaging what might be under the clothing. It stripped her.

"No peekie!" she scolded, feeling on safer ground, suddenly. The interplay between a man and woman on equal territory was a comfortable place to be. She knew that game fairly well. "Naughty boy!"

"Can't blame me! You're breathtaking!"

She flushed at his suddenly serious expression as he fairly stared into her soul.

"I'm just a girl!" she said, then quickly added: "No. I'm a woman who…isn't all that special, I suppose, except to myself and friends and…"

"Consider me a friend. Please. Tell me all!"

"Oh, you are clever! You got me there."

"I hope I get you wherever!" he chuckled. "Which puts me in the 'I'll settle for what ever you'll toss my way' like a little puppy dog."

"Now you sound pitiful."

"I certainly hope not!" He reached out and took her hands in his. "Just tell me whatever you want. I really want to know you better."

He felt warm around her fingers, stroking them ever so gently. She smiled, then withdrew her hand.

"You felt nice," he said, disappointed sounding.

"So did you. That's why … anyway. My life is rather dull stuff. Don't know why you should want to know anything about it." She was talking too fast, the words sputtering out. "Small town girl out to take the Big City on. That's me. And I've learned the Big Boys play by different rules here than they did back home."

"That tough?"

"Well, you should know. A billion lights on Broadway!"

"This ain't no Broadway. Just Hollywood."

"Just? Hollywood is the world!" she said. "Well, maybe the other way around—it isn't a place any more, is it? More an idea. But the industry…it can be tough on somebody starting out like me. I suppose you've heard that story to death."

"Not by such a charming lady."

"Oh, come on, Gene. I'm not silly enough to believe I'm so different."

"But you are. Believe me!"

"Sure, of course. You're sweet."

"Don't underestimate me, I can be horrid!"

"Horridly flattering."

"Maybe just horridly honest."

"But you been around!"

"Sure." He nodded. "Now stop avoiding and tell me about yourself."

"Dull stuff after what you do for a living. Alice Palmer!"

"Now that's dull stuff. Really."

"I'm just a girl. Looking for her first break in the movies."

She looked directly into his eyes as she said it. Her lips smiled as she tried to make it look like he was the one she hoped would help her. Not that she really believed he would be the one; but if *he* thought that's what she believed, then he'd be more than willing to "string her along"; and in the meantime she'd get a chance to meet other important people. But he would be her first leap across the fine casting couch divine—if it came to that.

The decision had been made, internally, and, strangely, it didn't seem such a horrid idea.

Connie wondered what had kept her from taking this new approach before. It wasn't morals. She was sure of that. Just her blind determination to get ahead on talent alone; to prove herself to herself. That was probably it. But now that she had started in a new direction she could see so many possibilities opening for her.

In her first month in town a middle-aged female agent had told her: "All you do is make a man think he's playing you along, while all the time you're doing the string-ing." Sure, she would have to give out a little. But what would be really wrong with that? Connie rationalized. She liked men. She liked sex. And she knew it wouldn't be too hard to wind a guy up; after that he was supposed to want more! That was the smart plan!—at least, that was the theory she'd decided act on. "Honey," a rather experience young acting coach had suggested: "Make a nice guy with connec-tions want more than a second round—and you're the driver; but let him think he's doing the seducing and sitting in the power seat."

A tired old game many successful women had learned to master.

Such advice had been freely offered, but she had refused to listen. Now she felt differently. And that gave her a strange sense of power.

"Say... What happened?" he inquired, dragging her thoughts back to the present.

"Oh, I'm terribly sorry. I just got to thinking." Connie smiled again, then reached her hands over to his; a second later they were clasping and intertwined with his fingers. "Where was I?"

"A girl looking for her first break in the movies."

"Oh, yes." She let her eyes fall downward, toward the empty cocktail glass. "It's pretty hard for a girl—you know."

He nodded as she looked up once more.

"I mean...the money—and the trying to get that first break. I don't get it—really! A person has to have a job to get experience, but experience to get a job. If you don't have the experience you can't get the job. Without the job, how can you get the experience?"

This was a direct appeal for him to help her and he fell right into the trap. His fingers squeezed hers as he looked deep and honestly into her eyes.

"There are ways. I mean...well, I've been known to help a damsel in distress..." His voice faded out.

She forced a happy smile, raising her eyebrows. "You really think you might be able to help me?"

"Well, that all depends," he vaguely offered. "All depends."

She knew what that meant. And she knew, also, that she had won the first round; but the game had at least 14 rounds to go and he wasn't stupid. In fact, damned smooth in his indirect manner. He had obviously played this game many times before.

Another couple of cocktails and an excellent steak dinner was followed by a tour of several night spots.

Then the promised Don Bagley was announced by the drummer conductor of the small combo. He was introduced as a special guest: "This is a man who has been at the top of his profession for many years, playing bass with such big bands as Stan Kenton, Les Brown and even with his own groups. Over the years he's been a standard professional, arranger and player. And now we're pleased to have him sitting in for a few numbers. Here's basically Bagley? Don Bagley on bass!"

The man played throughout the set with a soft selling musical line that played the swingingest jazz-on-the-rocks that anybody ever had the pleasure of hearing. And to add to the evening, giving a little more spice to it, he came to their table afterwards.

Eugene Bass seemed to know everybody.

Already things were beginning to look up. It amazed Connie to think what she had been doing to her so-called career in the past months. So much time wasted! From now on, every second was going to be spent in selling and buying her way up the ladder to fame and her name in big lights.

After the last stop, the last drink and the last dance, Eugene Bass suggested that they go over to his place for a nightcap.

She knew what that meant, and without hesitation grabbed at this chance to "close the deal" with a petty nice fella with connections. Even if he didn't pay off, it was a start down a new, more successful road to fame.

She had to start someplace and this man was not at all a bad beginning.

CHAPTER→❺

The next morning was a hang-over for Peter Denton. In more than just one way. What had started out to be a few pleasant days with a lovely doll by the name of Judy Grant had changed to a hellish nightmare with one problem after another.

The moment he had gotten to his apartment after seeing Miss Palmer there had been that phone message. All that he could do was pick up the studio cell and call Van Horn. He was put directly through to the man.

"What the hell did you tell that slut, Sweetheart?" Van Horn's voice shouted over the receiver. "What the hell did you say to her?"

"Nothing more than you suggested."

"Well, get your ass on down here. And quick! Our little Leading Lady and Eugene Bass are on their way here right now."

That was enough. He hung up. Told Judy.

"What does that man want now?" she complained in a high-pitched voice, quite obviously annoyed. "Honey, I guess you have to jump when he snaps his fingers. But …we just get started and…this has turned out to be some dump of a party!"

"Easy. 'Tain't my fault. Lousy business this is, and you shouldn't be in such a hurry to get sucked in."

"Well, this time you can take me along!" she determined, kissing his cheek. "Maybe he'll consider me for a part in the film. About time you yanked that idea across his brain cells."

"This is hardly the time."

"Never will be if you keep letting chances slip past

me. Why not just slip me in under the door?" She smiled sweetly, and for a moment he wasn't sure if the woman might not be serious. They enjoyed one another, but even Judy certainly had a limited supply of favors to hand out free of charge. Business was business. And he didn't fool himself about this young actor. A smart enough lady to know when to yanked the plug if a relationship wasn't paying off for her career. Some women could be strung along forever; stupidly so. Judy might like him, even a lot, might even be in "love" with him a little—he sorta guessed this could be true. She was nice, different than most, and certainly great kicks. But even real feelings would hardly mean much against a chance to get ahead in her career. Both of them were pretty realistic about that fact.

He tried to argue her out of it, but it didn't do any good. One thing that he had learned about Judy Grant was that once she made up her mind about something there was no stopping her. She might have to wait in the outer office, but if that's what she wanted to do, so be it. She made him promise to try opening the Van Horn studios doors to her.

"Just a mention to the man," she suggested. "Say, oh, I have somebody out there who would like to meet you. Or…mind if I give my lady a small walk on? Anything, Peter. I really do love being with you, but I have my pride and need more parts—the cost of living is very high!"

As expected the secretary had stopped her and she had been forced to wait in the reception room. He had warned her there was very little chance of getting past the woman. She sat down in the small chair, arranging the red dress to offer the best display of her body and picked up a magazine to read. She would be there when he was finished with business.

The next few hours had been hellish ones for Denton. But several immoveable facts revealed themselves. Alice Palmer was getting a better contract and twenty-four hour protection at the studio, at her home—and any place she might wish to go.

"And if anything—just *anything* goes wrong," she threatened in a tight voice, looking from one to the other of the three men, "then you'll wish to hell you'd never tangled with me!"

"Dearie," Van Horn cried in that sweet-sounding silk he always used for a voice when trying to con people into his way of thinking. "What in the world are you talking about?"

"Don't crap me!" she yelled back in a violently over-emoted tone. "You want me in this damn cheap movie of yours because of my *Big Name!* Cheap producer using Big Name Star to make money for him! You got a sweet deal with me, but don't get too wise!"

"You little tramp!" he snarled in contempt.

"Nothing little about me, Van boy!" she snapped, ignoring the insult.

The man blinked and continued: "Without that whoring body you wouldn't have made your first B picture."

"I'm not a dumb blonde. Mr. Horny! I know what sells. That's why I'm here, why you want me!"

"Sluts like you are a dime a dozen!" He dismissed her with a wave of his hand. "Don't kid yourself. Talent is cheap. And Big Boobs are common surgery gifts from hack docs! And expensive though they might be, little lay-dee, every cheap whore gets them if they want to remain in business. Don't think I'm stupid, Sweetheart!"

There was a long silence after that. Alice Palmer's face whitened slightly but she kept control of herself. The expression that crossed her features revealed the inner conflict her mind must be going through. She realized that what Van Horn just said was completely true.

"I think you might apologize for that!" she said in a sweet but tightly strained voice. "Mine are untouched by any cutman!"

He tossed his hands in the air in a grand movement, letting them freeze in space above his head. "But, Sweetheart, Darling—"

"Don't give me that sweet-darling routine!" She was strangely all soft voiced and actually almost amused looking as she studied the man. "We can be reasonable about this. All I'm concerned with is just a few simple things!"

The two were magnificently matched hard-lined pros enjoying every rich moment of the scene. Both of them were totally involved in the melodramatics, like to prima donnas doing a superbly crafted dance—one they had play-acted so many times in the past that neither recognized it as a well-mastered mockery of reality.

And they had seemingly forgotten the harsh exchange of insults. They were back where they'd started. Two hard-nosed pros fencing a skilled match of wits.

She continued: "One: protection from whomever wrote that note. Two: a percentage cut of the film along with a bump in my weekly paycheck!"

"Are you quite certain that's enough?" Van Horn countered almost too sweetly.

"And if anything happens that even looks like an attempt on my life—I'm out!" she finished.

"Oh, come on, Sweetheart, you know there's no reason on earth to even be fearful about that note. Just a crank!"

"Oh, go fly up a flagpole!" she screeched, stomping out of the office. "That's the deal. Take it or leave it!" her voice sounded as the door slammed shut behind her.

The moment the door closed, Van Horn turned toward Denton, "Look here, Mr. Trouble Shooter! All I can say is you had better see to it she has no reason—*none what so ever!*—to think anybody has made any attempts against her life. I mean that! If she walks out—you're through!"

It didn't seem to bother him that it wasn't Denton's fault. But that was Hollywood. Somebody had to be the fall guy, and Denton was number one on the list. He had once known a cameraman who had said: "I like to have a helper around so that if anything goes wrong I can blame him..." And *that* was Hollywood!

The moment Denton stepped out into the reception room he could see new trouble heading his way. Judy Grant was sitting quietly, waiting for him. He had actually forgotten her. Though she was outwardly calm, the temper was steaming inwardly. She walked out of the building without saying a word. But the moment they were in his car the explosion took place.

It started simple enough: "So you didn't ask him about a part for me?"

Her voice was light and seemingly innocent, but he couldn't help read the threat behind the words. She sounded determined.

"This wasn't the time. I warned you!"

"I don't know anything of the sort!"

"I told you..."

"You told me that there would be a part in this movie for me! That's all I know! You screwed me royal—for what? Fun and games? That's no deal breaker for me!"

Denton turned toward Judy and reached for her shoulders. But she struggled from his grasp. "No. Peter. I'm serious!"

"Come on, baby, don't be silly," he exclaimed, turning his attention to the car. They were driving Hollywood Boulevard as he said: "You should know better than this. You haven't been in this town that short of time ..."

"I was born here, Peter! So I do know the score. And the runaround, too! If you want me, I get a part. Cold but…that's the way it is. Right?"

"I thought we were more than just a business deal!" he offered, even surprised by his own words. But he actually did like her quite a bit. A fun companion.

"We are. But business is business. We have to sort things out, Peter. I'm not getting younger. I can't just play and wait forever. And I'm not a tramp! So … let us be realistic. If not, we better drop this whole relationship. Right now!"

For a long moment he remained silent. Then, biting his lower lip, he turned for a second and looked at the girl sitting beside him. *What kind of woman was she? There just wasn't any real reason for her acting up right then…Unless she was timing it like a clocked bomb. Taking the chance— any chance—to cut off the hot play before it got serious!*

"What brought this on?" he demanded, controlling the temper in his voice. "We've been so great together. I think you're special."

"Oh don't hand me that line!"

"I'm not handing any line!'

"The least you could have done was get something for me by now. I realized that while I waited there for two screaming hours! And that was some sight: Miss Palmer strutting out of that office with such a pleased smile on her face! I decided right then, a woman had to know when to cut bait or cut a deal! Whatever happened in that office it was obvious who had won. She actually gave me a quick smile, said *'don't let the horny man shit in your face! No winning there!'* Well…she's right!" She smiled very prettily up at him. "See what I mean?"

Furious at Alice Palmer, at Van Horn, and now at himself *and* Judy, he wanted to hit something.

"You aren't the only woman around!" he announced angrily, turning at the next corner and then heading the car in the direction of her apartment, "You're all a dime a dozen!"

"Think so?" she challenged, coldly. "Some dimes a better than others!"

He knew it was true. You couldn't get women like Judy Grant without a lot of work. A lot of work had gone into getting where he was with her. Now it was all blowing up because she couldn't wait a little longer. What did she expect him to do? Hold the old man down and tell him that he had a girl who wanted a part in a movie? Not right now. Not while his job was so dangerously hanging by such a thin string that could be cut by just one word from Van Horn or a wrong action from Alice Palmer.

One thing he did know: when Calvin Van Horn said something that was *exactly* what the man meant. He could make and break people in Hollywood. He would break Peter Denton if Alice Palmer blew his cork once more. And there wasn't anyway Denton could really keep the woman from doing just that.

The simple fact was: Van Horn wanted Alice Palmer to be in the picture. He didn't want any problems. He wanted things to run smoothly. In other words:

She had to be off his back!

If Denton couldn't get some of these problems smoothed out then he wasn't worth his weekly pay check, which was plenty high.

"Look, Judy, can't we…back off on this?"

"What's there to back off on? I think you're super nice. Really. Don't kid yourself about that. But enough is enough. You jump to his tune."

"Its my job."

"I understand that, Peter. I do. Really. Still, we might as well be realistic about all this. You have a problem. Resolve it. And then we can talk about us" She glanced meaningfully at him, quite serious. "I think we are special. In our way. Not many guys are as nice as you. Really, I mean it. But…I can see you have a tough problem here—and quite frankly I have things I have to do, too!"

"We can work something out, I promise you," he said, wanting to escape totally into her arms and forget Alice Palmer and Van Horne and the whole crappy problem. "Let's just pick up where we were stopped. I could use that kind of diversion."

"No. You need to stick to business. I'm certain."

"I need a hole in my head!" he cried, frustrated. "Come on, give me a break! It's been a bad scene."

"No! Not until you start playing fair with me! Until then, you can just forget that I exist!" She actually leaned over and gave his cheek a friendly peck with her soft, warm lips. "If that's possible!"

The bloody woman was playing him.

She continued in a very reasonable voice, even softly shaded on the warm side: "Come on, darlin', neither of us are innocent kids. We know the rules. And we know what counts. And we've both had a frustrating night of it! I'm exhausted. And quite frankly fed up with…everything! For now, anyway. You got to give a girl a break, for now."

A painful hurt went through his gut. "Okay, baby, if that's the way you want it!"

"Not the way I want it, the way things are," she simply said. "Now be a nice guy and do as I said. Home, James. Mine, not yours!"

He didn't want to lose Judy Grant. She was one woman he didn't like to think as a studio tramp, handed out from one man to the next. He suddenly decided she really was rather special in her way.

So there was nothing that he could do about it but be a gentleman. Half an hour later he was in a bar, drinking whiskey and using his cell to call all the women he knew.

A complete blank followed.

Nothing. No women. Nada.

No sex. *Nothing!*

So he drank some more. Until blackness had clouded over his vision and the next thing he knew he was getting up out of bed. And that damn hangover.

One hell of a hangover!

CHAPTER → 6

Connie's emotions were mixed and unsettled the next morning, after her date with Eugene Bass. She had no shame or guilt about what had happened. Surprisingly enough there really wasn't much to it. Not that they hadn't enjoyed one another. Simply that she felt somewhat casual about what took place. Part of what she was feeling had to do with a sense of conquest; and that was a little strange, because most people normally thought of *men* doing the conquering. Yet it was the woman who willingly submitted to her lover and thus was the seducer; not the male. No, it was something other than the feeling of victory.

She had *no* deep emotional feelings for Eugene Bass, even though he had been good enough in bed. And was a nice guy. But then, many men were good enough in bed, if they weren't brutes—and Bass was far from that. He had a certain amount of artistic care about the way he took a woman. She had liked that. So, even though there wasn't any emotion or "feeling" in her reactions toward the man, there had been a delightful thrill of excitement. That might have been part of her confusion; the knowing that she had liked it.

The apartment was nice, expensive, the furnisher classy dark oak trimmed. The walls held bright modern pictures.

He had first fixed a couple of drinks. Whiskey on the rocks. Put the lights on low, and some background music from the CD player. Everything was made to be a romantic interlude, instead of just some cheap *"strip and jump in bed, Darling!"*

For that she was thankful. It showed that the man had a lot of consideration for her feelings, even if he might figure her an easy conquest. That fact didn't really bother her because it was the "effect" she wanted to have on him. Make the guy think he was playing her along and things would might get the desired results.

The music played in the background. The whiskey burned through her system—heating every nerve. The lights added to the romantic setting. And the conversation was directly to the point—which was actually having nothing to do with sex.

They talked about everything *but* sex—but the mood was sensual and seduction seemed to be standing out like a distorted monster because of its invisibility.

She really couldn't remember what they had talked about—it wasn't that important. She was only aware that they were sitting close to each other, his arm around her shoulder. Really rather nice. Gene was a warm human charmer. By then she was well on her way to floating under the effects of the drinks. She had been tipsy for several hours, and the whiskey ran through her system like liquid fire.

The first pass was slow in coming. There was nothing crude about it, nor pushy in his manner. Just a gentle hand on her thigh. Then his fingers started working carefully along the inner surface and she couldn't control the sigh of intense pleasure breaking past her lips. It really felt good. And she couldn't remember how long it had been since a man had touched her in such a manner. Or even how long since she'd enjoyed a man's body.

Connie was surprised how responsive her nerves and flesh was to such a touch. Even more shocked at the swift blanket of overwhelming desire that flooded all her senses.

A convulsive tremble ran through her. Then she felt his hand slip under her dress. At the same time he pulled her closer, brushing his lips against hers. A moment later felt his tongue probe deeply as searching fingers stroked down her throat and finally lower along her side. She thrilled to the touch and kiss and she curled closer to him as other hand pulled down the front of her dress, cupping the fullness there. She trembled to his eager caress. Her breasts responded instantly, the nipples tight and hurting.

48

"Oh, Connie," he moaned as the kiss momentarily broke. "I've wanted to do that all evening!"

She smiled, shivering against him. "What stopped you?"

The line was a line. Almost like following some dumb, cheap script. But the dialog just fell into stupid line, so naturally that she couldn't help smiling in amusement.

"You laughing at me?" he murmured, not even caring if she were.

"Hardly," Connie assured him. "You feel nice, Gene. Really you do."

Again Connie felt like that was from some cheap flick.

"Not quite as nice as you do!" he chuckled, the palm of his hand giving her breast a meaningful squeeze to underscore his point. "I don't have one of those!"

She looked down at his groin. "And I..." she offered with a throaty laugh, "don't have one of those..."

"Thank god!" he laughed, delighted by her verbal counterpoint. He kissed her cheek, whispered: "If you did...I'd be in big trouble!"

"Well, maybe better not give me one!" she laughed throatily. "But I was so looking forward to you...well, sharing yours with me...just for the night."

"Oh, by God, she's has a wicked, sharp tongued mind! You could write cheap scripts, my little lady!"

"Is that suppose to make me hot and bothered?"

Then all hell broke loose!

He pulled her to him, and it was just a matter of a few short moments before they stretched out full length, locked against one another—unable to control the desperate grinding actions of their bodies which simply devoured one another in a shower of caressing kisses that drove them beyond sanity. She never knew when he became a part of her. It just happened as they surged together into one unified movement that continued without rest until they were both exhausted.

Later, around five in the morning, he had taken her to a small restaurant which stayed open twenty-four hours a day, and they'd had one of those quickie breakfasts. An hour later she was at her own apartment. But the important thing was the last words they had exchanged.

They were still in the car and she had told him not to bother taking her up. He just nodded. "When will I see you next?"

"I guess that's up to you, isn't it?" she had smiled back,

He thought for a moment and then said, "Tomorrow night?"

That had been good enough. In fact, it was almost perfect.

But she couldn't put her finger on the emotion which was jabbing at the back of her mind now as she sat down at the breakfast table to a cup of coffee.

She had made her point. She was heading in the right direction But it was still difficult to decide if she was happy or not. The main thing, though, she realized, was that the road was now clear—it was just a matter of continuing on down it. Regardless of where it took her, she was committed. There would be no backing down. No turning around. If she wanted to get a start in the movies, she would have to continue in this direction...

Maybe that was it.

Now she realized that was *exactly* what had been bothering her. It had nothing to do with submission or conquest; it had nothing to do with joy or sorrow; it had nothing to do with fear and bravery. It was a simple little thing which always bothers a girl when she has taken a gigantic step forward: for better or worse, she had made a decision which she'd have to stick by.

And right now she couldn't help but wonder if it had been the correct decision. She couldn't help wondering what changes it might make in her personality and outlook on life. She didn't want to become hard and cold; unemotional. She didn't want to lose the gentle, tender and sensitive side of herself. But somewhere deep down in her subconscious she was afraid something had died the night before. That something had been squeezed out of existence by a hard cold core which would now start growing like a cancer; reshaping her whole personality to something alien and hard.

A cold shiver ran through her delicate frame. There

50

wasn't anything she could do about it now. Everything she had done and would do and become was a part of her which she would have to live with for the rest of her days.

All these feelings had nothing to do with Gene. He was simply a symbol of things yet to come.

She needed someone to talk to. She had to do something other than just think things out by herself. Maybe she should go over to Judy's place...

Judy and Connie had always gotten along well together and it might be fun to see her old roommate now. Yes, she liked the idea. Some time had passed since they'd really visited together—and she missed seeing Judy, even if the girl had changed a lot recently.

Something had made Judy change from a nice, kind-hearted, young girl, to a frustrated woman who would do anything to get ahead in show business. All over night, it seemed.

Shaking herself, she forced those thoughts away. Regardless of what Judy had turned into professionally, she was still fun socially. They had been good friends for a while and Judy was the only person she was able to really talk to quite frankly—and there were very few secrets between them.

Maybe a sunning at the beach. Judy liked to lie in the sun.

She reached for her cell and dialed the other girl's number.

"Hello," she heard a sleepy voice murmur over the receiver.

"Hi, Judy, this is Connie."

"Hi, Con—what's up?"

"Nothing...say, are you doing anything this afternoon?"

The other girl seemed to think for a moment and then said, "Nothing—that darn Denton is off my list right now...until he comes through with a part!"

"Oh, no!" Connie cried in sympathy. "I thought things were hot between you two!"

"Sure. Very hot. He's super in bed. But ... even if a girl likes him, and that's easy enough to do with Peter Denton...well, there has to be limits!"

"You sound down."

"No. Just pissed. These Hollywood creeps! I've been around this town all my life—been trying to get into the business ever since I could remember. And all a girl gets is a roll in bed. Well—damn it all, I got other plans!" The girl laughed and then continued. "Things aren't as dead as Mr. Peter Denton seems to think."

"What's that mean?"

"Well, I have plans for him! You know Vic Bolton?"

"No—not exactly."

"He's a writer. Been doing the script for the new Alice Palmer movie. Denton is the assistant producer for the pic. Well—don't let this get any further—"

"I won't—promise!"

"Well, Vic is doing what he can to help me get a part. He's working on Denton, Van Horn and everybody. We've been friends for years. He's the guy who introduced Denton to me—so you see...Mr. Peter Denton is about to get a little surprise. As it is, I got him exactly where I want him! A real player when it comes to a smart woman."

"What's the beef, then?"

"He refuses to move fast enough...I played my main card yesterday and—well, I suppose he has issues. But...I played and I think I'll win. It'll just take a bit of time. He'll have to get me a screen test, first, of course. But I'll get a part or else!"

"Well, can you really expect a contract right off!"

"Well, maybe? Why not?" Judy's voice sounded uncertain. "I've been working my body to death letting Hollywood creeps slobber all over me! I figured Pet to be different. And it looked like he was. And maybe he is. We'll see."

There was a silence after that and then Connie took the chance to again suggest that they get together.

She didn't really know whether to be depressed or happy. Hearing about Judy and what the girl had said was a little depressing. In a way, she didn't know if she wanted to be with her all day. But it was too late now to do anything about it.

What difference did it make? she thought, getting into her bathing suit. They would lie on the beach, talk—like they always did—and…

      Maybe she'd learn about how a girl really puts something over on the Hollywood Casting Couchers.

CHAPTER→

If the day before had been a painful problem, the one he now faced was even worse for Peter Denton.

The Palmer woman.

And then Judy Grant. That was one of the first thoughts that bothered him as he poured a cup of coffee for himself. *Maybe he should call the girl; she might have changed her mind.*

But that wouldn't do any good, he realized. When Judy made up her mind about something, that was that! Regardless of anything else. Plus, maybe she was just playing him for a sucker—that wouldn't be surprising. She was hardly stupid.

The only thing he couldn't understand was that she had one moment been all love and kisses and the next, cold ice. The chill was stark; unexpected. Did it reveal something about her that wasn't quite obvious when being teased by her charming body and seductive madness?

Maybe it had been the waiting in the office. That could have been part of it. They had been in Van Horn's office with Miss Palmer for a long time—at least a couple of hours. No wonder she had gotten mad. Yet, it had been Judy's idea to come along.

Another thought occurred to Denton. Maybe she had just flared up for the moment and then been forced to continue. She might be thrilled to have him call. Things certainly might look different after a good night's sleep.

He grabbed his cell, which was placed within easy reach of the breakfast table, and dialed her number.

Her sleepy voice sounded in his ears. He said, "Hi, baby. Pete here."

54

"You!" Her voice was biting. "What now?"

She had changed: and it didn't do any good to their relationship that he had called her. It would make her think that she still had the upper hand; that she had won.

He thought quickly, trying to dream up some way to save face. No good to let her have the upper hand. The only way a man could win was to play it smart.

He had made one fatal mistake: he'd given in to impulse at the wrong time; and now he had to find some way out. Think fast and come through with quick answer.

"Are you still there?" Judy's voice asked. A slight air of interest showed through, even though she was doing her best to remain cool.

"Sure...I'm sorry, I have a lot of things on my mind right now," he lied.

"Well, then, what the hell did you call me for?"

"I have good news, baby."

"What?" The astonishment of that one word, and all the emotion which was backing it up, made him almost hate himself for what he was about to say.

"Sure, baby. I finally got a chance to talk to Mr. Van Horn. He said he'd see what he might do!"

Her words were chilled. "Put me right on the fast track! I see!"

"Come on, baby. What else can you expect?"

"A contract! Is that expecting too much?"

"Be reasonable."

"That's what I've been doing. Being reasonable. And where has it got me? Tell me that! Where?"

He didn't have any answer for that, because the only thing that he could possibly say was it had landed her in bed with him. For a moment he felt a slight pain of regret that he hadn't really played fair with her. Yet, on the other hand, he *did* actually plan on trying to help her. "It's gotten you a part, baby. What else do you want?"

"A *part?*" her voice screamed in delight. Then it sobered, slightly. "What kind of part?"

That was the million dollar question! He couldn't dream up another lie to support the first one. Yet, she had him hooked with that direct question. "Well, look, baby. He just said he'd fix you up. He didn't say *what* part...you know how it is. A part is written in a hundred ways to get you in— just take it easy! They'll whip something up just for you."

"When's the screen test?"

That was another direct and pointed question. It was an honest one. "He didn't say—exactly."

"When he does, you can call me up!"

The line went dead.

That did that.

He was finished with Judy just when things had been getting along pretty well; just when they were developing to the stage he wanted and had been working for these last weeks together.

Damned! I really like her! He had to admit to himself.

"Plenty of willing bods out there, Pete," he muttered, angrily. "They're all the same. Poke 'em hokum!"

Despite himself he had to laugh at that horrid pun. "Well, Pete, you have more serious problems to deal with."

To Hell with her!

No, he realized, *she was something worth the effort!* All he would have to do was to get that part for her, set up a screen test. How hard would that be? Not as hard as her lovely young body was able to make a man feel.

"God, Pete, you're hoary as hell!" And Judy had run his motor up twenty notches and left it out to dry last night. She had really strung him out!

He downed the rest of the now cold coffee and then went to the bathroom. After a hot shower he dressed and then poured himself a shot of whiskey. The liquor went down in one gulp. The morning routine was over; now he was ready for a rough day at the studio.

Somehow he would have to arrange to set up a screen test for Judy. He didn't know for sure how that could be done. Maybe if he shifted a few schedules and shuffled a few people around.... It was dirty business; but if he wanted to make Judy happy—*then he'd have to do a little honest work to get her!*

Half an hour later he was parking his car in his private place on the lot of *Van Horn Studios.* This was going to be one of those days, he *knew* it. The first day after a three day week-end was enough to make anybody wish that the work week was finished rather than beginning.

Alice Palmer had to be top of his list.

Betty, his secretary, handed him a memo note. "Miss Palmer left this message. Called early."

"Okay, thanks...anything else—more up-lifting?"

"Gene Bass called. Wants to see you. For lunch?"

"Nothing else on the schedule?"

"It's blank."

"Okay. Pencil him in. I'll look into this Palmer bit. Put a call through to her."

A few minutes later, in the privacy of his office, Denton had Alice Palmer on the line.

"What is it, dear?" he asked in his most professionally silky voice.

He didn't feel in the mood to be pleasant to this little bundle of headaches.

"I've been reading this damn script!" she screamed at him.

"What is it this time?"

"It has me dressed in rags. That's no way to show off the famous Palmer figure!"

"But you're crossing the Rockies. You can't..."

"And no makeup!"

"But..."

"What kind of writer do you have here?"

"He's considered top of the line."

"Oh, crap! Either you change that—or I'm out!"

She hung up.

Women seemed to be hanging up on him all the time today. It just wasn't his morning.

A second later, Betty called through the inter-com. "There's a Mr. Brown here to see you."

"What's he?"

"Van Horn sent him over."

He signed: "Okay, let him in."

The phone rang. It was Davis: sets. He had a financial problem. By the time Denton had okayed an extra allotment to the man's department, the "Mr. Brown" was in front of him.

He carried a briefcase and had a lovely bleach-blonde woman at his side who sat in the large easy chair directly opposite Denton. Her body movements were fluid, sensual, and bluntly inviting. She seemed to be making it a point to lean forward so that he could see down her revealing neck-line. She wasn't wearing a bra and he saw far more than she might have wanted him to. No. He saw exactly what she in-vited him to stare at. Her eyes flashed hot. Her smile point-edly flirting with him.

Brown was an agent. He wanted to set up a screen test for his client. "Mr. Horn—I mean Van—said to see you."

Miss Gloria leaned over farther. "I sure would be *thrilled* at anything you'd do for me. I'll do whatever you need me to do, Mr. Denton. It would mean everything to me!"

Simply put that meant he could have her body here and now. He'd heard that pitch before. He'd taken it before. And she had a great body! He wondered just how much was her natural self, and not medically padded!

The face of Judy Grant blended over her features and he shrugged his shoulders. "Right now we're booked. Solid." He was speaking to the agent, but his eyes never left the woman's. "That is—things are pretty busy...tell you what. Leave her picture, credits and things like that. I guess you know the routine."

Brown nodded, shrugged his own shoulders and pulled out a large brown envelope from his briefcase.

The phone rang before the man could say anything.

"This is Bolton!" a voice yelled in his ears. It was the writer of the Palmer movie. He must have gotten the word from somewhere that the "Big Star" wanted script changes.

The headaches were beginning again.

"What's this bit about the changes?"

"Look, I'm busy right now, Vic. But, come on over in about twenty—no! You have anything planned for coffee break?"

"Okay, see you at ten or so."

"Right. Thanks, Vic."

The phone clicked.

Denton turned to the agent and the lovely over-heated starlet. "Well, just give all that information to my secretary."

Denton stood and extended his hand. That was the end of that—except as the agent was leaving the blonde stepped over to Denton. She moved in close. Almost touching him. Her eyes were bright and shining. Her lips parted slightly and she moistened them with her delicate pink tongue.

"You know, I'd be very thankful if you'd see what you can do for me. I mean, well, you know what I mean…" Her voice trailed off, but her eyes looked pointedly at him. The implication was not at in any way subtle.

"Here's my cell and email," she whispered, handing him a slip of paper. She let her hand slide down his arm, in a very generously casual manner, without comment. A warm threat of pleasure shot through him.

Then she left.

One thing he could say: she was sure brazen enough, and anxious enough, and willing enough, and sexy enough; and...

He pocketed the card she'd given him.

And maybe he might give her a call. Especially since Judy was giving him such a cool treatment.

Then he forgot all about her when the phone rang again.

This time it was costumes.

The normal routine of the day had begun and he could almost feel an ulcer starting to develop inside his gut.

His head already ached, and after a couple of aspirin he told Betty to call Mr. Van Horn's office. This was as good a time to see what could be done about a screen test for Judy as there ever would be. Try now and get it over with.

Van Horn wasn't in.

He thought for a moment and then made an important decision on his own: maybe he could arrange things without Van Horn's okay. It hadn't occurred to him before. The fact was that the man had sent this Miss—whatever her name was—to arrange a screen test. Van Horn wouldn't really know the difference if it was Judy Grant instead. Horn had no doubt already forgotten about the Mr. Brown and his sex pot client! There was a budget open to Denton. He'd just have to say it was the girl Van Horn had sent up to him.

A little shifting. A little shuffling. And Judy Grant would be satisfied and back into his arms.

He buzzed his secretary and told her to make arrangements for a screen test at the earliest possible time. Then he settled back and started studying the papers which were lying in his "In" box. That took care of him until ten. And then the second headache hit.

Victor Bolton was a temperamental writer who sometimes actually believed that his golden words were priceless, And for the price he was being paid it would seem that Van Horn bought the idea.

Bolton had blown his stack in two ways. During the time since Denton had spoken to him on the phone, the writer had managed to get slightly loaded.

And that's all Denton needed!

"Nobody changes a word!" the writer had cried out in heated determination.

"What's gotten into you, Vic? You never used to be this way. A real commercial hack."

"Well, things have changed. They have changed for *Victor Bolton!* They can't stay the same way all the time. Now, can they?"

"No, I guess not. But, I sure wish you'd be a buddy. Just this one time. We've got problems enough with Miss Palmer. Don't add to them!"

"Hell, I'm not adding. It's the Palmer hag! She wants to change a realistic scene into a Hollywood glamour sex-gag. I won't have anything to do with it. *Nothing!* Understand?"

"Look, isn't there some way to work things out?"

"Nothing! Change that scene and you go get another script writer! I don't mind a few words here and there—that's to be expected! But this. It's going too far. This changes the whole meaning of the picture. The whole idea of pioneers. They didn't go out west with beauty kits. At least, not the kind of woman that Miss Palmer will be playing. Only the cheap whores and tramps wore any kind of makeup

60

in the way that she wants to be dolled up."

"Look, Vic. Can't you play along?"

"Nothing! That scene stays the way I wrote it or you can get another 'hack'!"

There was a silence for a long time after that, then Bolton took a deep breath. "I don't know why you guys didn't use Judy Grant when I suggested her to you."

"When was that?" Denton asked, not really paying attention to what the writer was saying.

"Oh, I told blow hard Horn she was perfect for the part and he blew his cork." Bolton shrugged his shoulders. "Guess you weren't around—that's right! I talked to Van Horn about it around six months ago.

"He wanted a big name star. *Hell!*—Judy would have been perfect for the role!"

"She's unknown, Vic," Denton told him. "And who knows for sure she can act?"

"Come off it—Pete. Don't give me that crapola! Nobody knows how to act. The camera and lights and sound make an actor and actor—then with a little publicity you have a star. Who cares about acting. Just be yourself in front of the camera and let the film cutters make you look good!"

"Wish it were so."

"If it isn't then I'm Hemingway! And that I ain't no way! You guys make too much of talent. The talent isn't in the acting, just in the writing and cutting."

Denton shrugged. There was no used debating the issues. Writers always had over-size egos and thought they were the beginning and end. Maybe in books and such. But in Hollywood they were low rung on the creative flag to success. Everybody stomped on their words, from script typist to janitor. Writers offered up the beginning concept and actors, directors and all the rest, including producers and PR men, agents, secretaries, and anybody within easy reach of the script added their two-cent ideas. What ended on film was anybody's guess. But certainly not the writer's domain.

"Vic. Just do us all a favor and be a pro. We don't need any more shit hitting the fan!"

CHAPTER → 8

"What's the problem, Gene?" Peter Denton asked, looking at the studio press agent who was sitting across the small table. They were at one of the many Hollywood lunch restaurants. Both had martinis before them. The drink came with the price of the Cheeseburger Deluxe. Regardless of modern day no Cocktail Lunches on the expense accounts, both of them were quite willing to swill out hard bucks for quick drinks.

"Everything, in a way, Pete. Most particularly, Miss Palmer."

"You too?"

"Me, too? Hell, man, I'm the one who gets the headaches first! We're having repercussions about that note, already. At least half a dozen cranks have turned themselves in to the police, claiming they're the one who sent the letter. That's not our problem but this is!"

He handed Denton a note. "Take a look at it!"

The note was simple and direct and to the point:

"If Miss Palmer makes this picture with you it will never be completed."

"What kind of bull is this?"

Eugene Bass looked long and hard at Denton, his eyes narrowing slightly in concentration. "That's what we can't figure out. It arrived today by e-mail. Crank. Yes. How'd they get my e-mail addy? And why? Why this particular film? We aren't that important."

Denton felt his imaginary ulcer grind. More problems. More headaches. If it wasn't one thing, then it was another.

Now it was this new note that Eugene Bass found in

his e-mail. Denton looked from the message to Bass and then back to the computer printout. He read it over a couple of times and then smiled, "Just think of the press we could get out of this!"

"I was thinking all about that. It would help the movie a hell of a lot! That's for sure."

"I'd rather drop it into the trash bin!" Denton offered, tiredly. "This kind of thing is not good! If our Star finds out…*it'll finish us with Miss Palmer!*"

The silence grew heavy and depressing. The meal came and the two ate without a word. There just didn't seem to be much to say. All they could do was to keep totally quiet about the note.

"Say, you know Vic Bolton?" Denton asked, suddenly remembering the script writer problem.

"Sure."

He hadn't been asking a question so much as indicating a new direction for their. But he still felt silly having said it. "Well, Vic is turning out to be another problem. Palmer wants script changes to make her look more glamorous and Vic won't make them. You have a suggestion?"

Bass looked at him for a long time before he said anything. His face lined slightly, and then after lighting a cigarette he started speaking, slowly and carefully. "You have to understand the writer-mind. It has a long series of channels and devices and frustrations. With Vic it's a matter of both professional pride and a little bull-headedness."

"Hell, I know all that!"

"No! That's not exactly the way I meant it. What I mean is that with Bolton you have to approach him through an indirect means. Hit him from the side. He has a lot of pride when it comes to proving his ability to hack out a lot of crap. He also has a lot of pride when it comes to his 'arty' stuff. With this movie, he's confused a bit—from what I've been able to see. Wants to be arty—but that's a thing you can't be in the movies! Well not in a Horn film, that is. Still…it's that damn best-selling novel of his! It went to the guy's head!"

"That's no help!"

"Give me a little time. What I'm leading to is you'll

have to reach him in a way that will use that stubborn pride of his *against* him and *for* you. Don't fool around…"

The conversation was getting too deep for Denton. It was too stilted. He shrugged, motioned to the waiter and said: "Let's forget it for a moment. There's another problem I have that we might as well talk about. Something more personal. About—well, you've been around a little longer than I have...I mean, with Van Horn."

The waiter came then. Denton signed the bill and then he and Bass stood and started out of the restaurant. "This has to do with setting up a screen test.

Bass looked strangely at him. Then he smiled. "A girl of yours?"

"How'd you know?"

"Simple. When a new assistant producer comes into the business, there are a flock of girls around that want to get an *in* and he wants to get *into*. Simple?"

"Simple, I guess. But can I get away with it?"

"What do ya mean by that?"

"Let's say that I wanted to get a screen test for a girl I think has a lot of talent. Can I go ahead with it and then just not mention it to Van Horn?"

"Hell! Why not? It's done all the time. You'd better be sure what you're doing, though. What I mean is: she had better be worth the money—not just on the couch, either. In other words: if she's good, Van Horn won't care. And if she cheap and good, he'll be delighted. In case you were thinking about cost. I take it you want to do this on the sly—without verbal permission. So just be careful,"

"Another thing, Gene. I'm sorry about that conversation about Vic. I'd certainly consider it a favor if you could get him off my back."

The other man looked for a long time at the ground and then his eyes raised to meet Denton's. "See what I can do. Nothing promised, Just see what can be done,"

"Thanks."

They got into Bass' car and the press agent directed it into traffic. "About this girl of yours...have anything planned for the weekend?"

Denton thought that over. He didn't know about

Judy. Even with the screen test deal she might still be playing it cool. "What do you have in mind?"

"Well, I met this broad the other evening and we were out last night. Have another date with her tomorrow. Maybe something could be set up at the beach house for the weekend. If the girls are willing, that is."

Denton shook his head. "I don't think that's possible with Judy, I'm having a problem with her, right now. For a couple of days I'll have to be careful."

"Sorry about that. Maybe I could fix you up with something."

"Hey, wait a minute!" He dug into his pocket; his fingers nervously searching for a white slip of paper. "Maybe I do have something right here in the palm of my hand!"

He looked at the paper, reading it for the first time. It gave the bare facts: *Gloria@LaSota.com.* Then her cell phone number. The only thing necessary for him to do now was contact her.

"I'll give you a call, Gene. This is something new and, quite frankly a dish with a lot of flesh to be had."

"You guys—get all the luck!"

"I don't know about that. You're going great guns with the women, too. And, I might add, it's a free ride from *us* boys!"

"Hell! What does that mean?" the other laughed.

"We have the big deals to offer. All you pressmen do is know *us.* So...the girls hanker for our attention through you!"

The laugh sounded slightly forced then.

There was a lot of truth in what he had just said, Denton realized, *and maybe Gene's laugh was a little stilted.*

But the man still laughed.

Twenty minutes later Denton was talking over the phone to the lovely, voluptuous Gloria La Sota.

"Oh, *Mister Denton,"* she sighed over the receiver in a voice heavy with lush invitation. "I'd just *love* that. When will you pick me up?"

"Around eight, Friday evening."

"Fine. *Oh,* how *thrilling!* You won't regret it!*"*

He didn't plan on regrets in any way with this Gloria La Sota. Stagy though her name may be, and maybe even with implanted boobs, it sounded like she'd be a nice weekend squeeze. The woman left nothing to a man's imagination other than the promise of fulfilling his every fantasy.

Denton hung up and then called Eugene Bass. The arrangements were made. Then a few minutes after that his secretary told him the screen test had been set up for the next Monday. For a moment he thought that maybe he would call Judy and tell her himself; then he decided against it. Let it go through normal channels, Then she would call him up, all excited and willing to play the game *his* way. He'd have the upper hand. And that's the way he wanted it. Play the girls against each other. That was the best way to get ahead in this business of male and female relationships on the half couch. The hot, loving, fun making casting couch upon which all of the eager young players served complete meals of their bodies.

The rest of the afternoon was taken up in business conferences. Seeing a few daily rushes on the Palmer movie which were location shots taken that afternoon. Then a few action and FX shots dealing with a sci-fi picture with he had been asked to check out, even though he wasn't working on the film.

It was just another average day at the studio. Only spiced by the little more than average bust line and the promise of things to come Friday night. The lady would offer whatever he wanted on the slim chance it would help her career.

What a faked name! Gloria Smith or Brown or Jones was probably closer to the truth—that is, if her first name was even Gloria. But she'd probably be a Glori-ous delight!

Well, it didn't matter in the least to him. He planned on having one Glor-ified time—and that was all that *would* count.

He couldn't help smiling at the corny pun that had managed to flash through his mind while his eyes were supposed to be watching a *monster from outer space* ripping apart Los Angeles with its bare claws.

It would be fun "glorifying" Gloria. That was all he

could think of right then. His problem was that he still hankered for Judy—a finishing of their mutually nearly shared mating of their bodies the other night.

Or maybe it was because he didn't want to think of the headache of Alice Palmer and what she could very easily do to his career. If he couldn't keep her down, then, from Van Horn's point-of-view, he wasn't worth his pay check and would lose his job.

And then there was the concern about Judy. He was taking a terrible—and maybe foolish—chance for her and perhaps endangering his job in trying to set up a screen test. Of course it wouldn't come to Van Horn's attention unless he thought she was worth the effort. Actually one of his jobs was to screen any tests before they got to the Big Boss. There wasn't really much danger—unless it was discovered that he set Judy up for just one purpose—which had nothing to do with talent, or the forward growth of *Calvin Van Horn Productions, Inc.*

And that was the only danger...

He forced the face of Gloria to fade over his thoughts. Her large, big-busted body. Her big wide lips. Cheap, but sensual face. And brazen promise of a hot time in her arms.

Think about Gloria and he didn't have to think about the other problems.

Like getting on good terms with Judy again.

Gloria!

Only Gloria and her big boobs!

Be they real or fake, they'd be fun joys to enjoy.

CHAPTER→❾

Connie felt a mixture of excitement and depression as she drove in the large Cad next to Eugene Bass. The other couple was in the back seat. A Mr. Peter Denton and some little tramp called Gloria something-or-other. She didn't remember the girl's last name because she didn't consider it worth remembering. But the man: *Peter Denton.* That name hit home. As if she had heard it somewhere before. It was bothering her a little because she believed that it was somehow important that she remember where she'd heard it.

Still, that wasn't the thing which seemed really to be depressing her. It was the bleached blonde woman.

A little slut who sold her body just to get a chance at a few movie parts.

Just like *she* was doing. Just like the high and mighty Connie Remington was doing. And that was what bothered her—*a lot!*

She didn't like thinking of herself as being like that little whore sitting in the back seat. Sitting there in her white dress that seemed as cheap and dirty as the woman in it. The cloth clung to her over-developed body like another layer of silky skin.

Yet, Connie had to admit, her own dress was plenty tight. The only difference was that Connie's dress was more expensive, had more class and was definitely of better design and taste. That was the only consolation which she could think of.

There were other things that were bothering her, too. One was the place they were headed. She realized what was going to happen. Not that she didn't like Eugene Bass. In fact, she even looked forward to his caresses and love-making. But she didn't like the idea of "shucking up" in an all-out "week end orgy" like this was sure to turn into.

Of course it was to be handled with all the care and gentleness that was possible. Just a few drinks. Dancing. Dinner. Things like that. But only one fact stood out in bold-faced type:

SEX PARTY!

And even though Bass was being as nice about the it as he could, there weren't any bones being broken over what would happen.

They would have a few drinks. A dinner. And then more drinks. A little later in bed. It wasn't Gene, but rather the fact that the other two were there. It all made her feel kinda cheap.

Sex Party!

"What you thinking about?" Eugene asked, looking in her direction for a short second.

"Oh, nothing."

"Come on. You've been sitting there since we started out. Not saying a word. Anything bothering you?"

"No no, not really!"

She couldn't say how she really felt. Not with the others there. Not even to Bass. Most of all not to him.

Think about the beautiful ocean. The red setting sun. That was beautiful. Yes, that was much better! The ocean was stretched out to the red horizon, sky breathtaking in its clouded orange wonder.

The car came to a stop and she realized they had reached their destination.

"Okay, baby, here we are—all out that's getting out!" Bass cried, stepping from the car and running around to her side. He helped her out and for a moment she felt a certain security. The feel of his hand on her arm, and then his fingers as they reached for and intertwined with hers, all helped to make things seem a little friendlier. And they were friends, in a way.

"Gee, what a pad," Gloria cried in her high-pitched screeching voice. It grated on Connie's nerves but she held down the acid remark which was wanting to flip off the tip of her tongue. There wasn't any reason to take it out on the other woman. It wasn't Gloria's fault for being the way she was. Nor was it Connie's fault for being what she was. Maybe it had to do with the fact that she saw herself in Gloria. Not exactly herself; but what she was afraid of appearing in the eyes of others—what she might become, someday. And quite determined not to let happen.

God! She hoped, that would never happen!

She was determined never to be that kind of female. There must be a fine line between what Gloria represented and what she was offering. There *had* to be one; and she was determined to somehow find it.

The beach house was rustic in style. Just set up for such an arrangement as they now found themselves. An ideal romantic interlude or playhouse for wild parties.

High beam ceiling. A large home bar along one wall with a stereo set built in.

In a few moments the lights were low and the soft romantic music in the background. Drinks had been served all around.

The bar had four stools arranged around it and they seated themselves on them. After the first drink, the atmosphere became less stilted.

She had learned a little about Peter Denton. He was an assistant producer; the type of contact she really needed. And it was this kind of power-broker she should latch onto first chance she got! If it was possible. That reality was somewhat unnerving.

Then the second piece of information.

"Did you get that screen test set up?" Bass asked Denton, while at the same time working his fingers gently on Connie's arm.

"Oh, you mean with Judy?"

Judy...Grant? That jolted her. Who else could it be? She didn't hear the rest of that part of the conversation. Instead, she was trying to recover from her shock, for suddenly she knew where she'd head his name.

Peter Denton was the guy Judy had been running around with.

70

That knowledge made her very uncomfortable. It told so much, so fast. It revealed too much, too fast!

Judy had been working for months on this guy!

She'd bent over backwards—literally—to please him, so that she could get that "in" with the studios she'd been trying to get for years. Now Denton was running with another woman.

Typical. Maybe it didn't make any difference.

Not that that was wrong. It wasn't even any of her business. It was just that it made her feel suddenly cheap. It made her realize a little about the workings of the men who had the power of hiring and firing; of giving people breaks.

Oh, how they abused that and the women who ran through their offices, begging to get a break. Even nice guys. Maybe there really weren't any nice guys. Maybe it was all an illusion.

Denton couldn't have any actual intentions of getting this Gloria a screen test for any free favors with her body. The reference to a test for Judy was no doubt just a fool trick to impress the ladies of the evening—Connie and Gloria.

And now she was beginning to wonder if maybe she had made a mistake about Eugene Bass. In fact, she was sure it had been a mistake. But what could she do about it now?

"What's with you, baby?" Bass asked, concern clouding his features. "You've thought yourself to death all evening. Thinking can make a dull woman. Pep out of it! This is a time to be joyful; to have fun; cheer up!"

She tried to smile; and didn't find it too hard while looking into his eyes; in fact, she found it nice. Bass wasn't a bad sort really. At least he didn't seem to be into drugs. Just a man on the make. But what was really wrong with that? Women these days felt the only way they could get a man hooked was by using sex—but *not*, necessarily, letting the man have it. That was the trouble; women were afraid that all they had to sell was their bodies—and they made the price much too high.

There was more to relationships between people beyond sex. In fact, sex was a small part of it all. Caring. Tenderness. Sharing dreams. Even sharing long silences.

"When's food on?" she asked Bass.

71

Gloria answered rather crudely: "Here's all the food this girl needs!"

"Hungry?" Eugene inquired, first to answer Connie, then directed at the other too, also.

Peter Denton grinned, shrugged. "I'll eat anything you have to offer."

The woman's hands gripped at his arm. Her eyes were fairly feasting on him. "Will I fit the bill?"

The man looked uncomfortable, but managed a quick smile. His eyes flashed away from Gloria's and suddenly gazed right into Connie's and held there, as if frozen in a time lock.

She felt an electric flash whip up her spine. Her body literally tightened in reaction. A flush burned her cheeks and she felt stark naked. The man didn't look away, just continued to gaze right into her very soul, it seemed. A shiver rushed over her.

Gloria snipped, noticing that connection: "He's all mine, lovely lady!"

That shocked Connie out of her frozen hot state. "Oh, you're welcomed to him, really!"

She quickly glanced at Bass. "We should get something together, the two of us. *Food* I mean!"

"You didn't offer anything else!" he chuckled, taking her arm.

"I didn't want you to get the wrong idea about me, Gene," she murmured, letting herself brush up against him, rather intimately, a show of possession to flaunt into the other couple's face. "I'm a nice girl."

Gloria laughed loud at that. "I just bet you are!"

"And," Gene whispered to Connie, "you're good, too!"

"Thanks!" They moved into the kitchen, ignoring the other two.

The man shrugged, then moved toward the double doors that looked out on the ocean. Waves were breaking across the large rocks along the shore several yards below the house.

Denton's voice muttered, "Cut that out!"

Both Connie and Bass turned, surprised at the man's

statement.

Nothing obvious was evident. They appeared rather nicely locked in a rather intimate conversation, the woman's lips very close to his.

Connie shrugged, returned her attention to the man at her side. She looked into his eyes, pleadingly. For some reason she felt a kind of closeness to Eugene. It wasn't love or even a feeling of deep affection. It just boiled down to liking. She liked the man; but that was all!

One thing she kept reminding herself: never get emotionally attached to anyone; and she was safe with Eugene Bass.

"I can start things," he offered, leaning close to her and brushing his lips on her cheek,

"Not that way you won't!" she laughed. Strangely her voice sounded husky and deep even in her own ears. It must have sounded heavy with passion to Bass.

"Okay, then, let's get the meal started!" he suggested in a much too nervous manner. "Want to help?"

She didn't, but there wasn't anything else left for her, except join Denton and his sexy little "Gloria the whoria."

Oh that's horrid, she thought with a smile.

The man noticed, said: "What'd I say?"

"Nothing at all."

"Then why the smile?"

Impulsively she found herself telling him in a soft whisper.

He exploded with laughter. "God, your funny!"

"No I'm not!" she literally giggled like a little girl. "I'm horrid!"

"Well, horrid or not."

"Well, it wasn't nice."

"Well, quite frankly my dear, right on the nose, I'm afraid. Poor boy."

"Sure. Bet he's eating his heart out!"

"Hardly. But he's not into that kind of woman heart and soul."

"Does he have to be with...Gloria the..." She couldn't say the rest of it, but laughed instead. "Well that kind of woman?"

For a moment they were awkwardly quite, each somewhat uncomfortably aware of some under-lying meaning to her words.

"You're not like her, Connie," he finally announced, very seriously, as if reading her thoughts.

"I hope not! I'd hate to think you believed so."

"I don't!" Then opening the frig, he said, "Here, catch!"

He tossed her a head of lettuce. "Think that'll be enough for all of us?"

"Depends on what goes with it," she countered, lightly.

"Well..." the man's eyes raced over her. Then he crossed them very dramatically, grinning like an idiot. "Would I do for a main snack?"

"Actually, Gene, if you'd uncross those eyes and help me with the salad we might be able to serve up a meal in short order."

"Good idea. I have some frozen pasta up there. Whack it into the microwave and we have a hot dinner for the four of us!"

They were silent for a moment. Then realized how quite things were in the other room.

He grinned. "What do you think? Are they or aren't they?"

Connie had to laugh at that. "Maybe they are, maybe they aren't."

"Wanna bet?" he challenged.

"Not on your life, darlin'!" she said, taking the large knife out of a rack and whacking it into the lettuce now on the chopping board.

"Hey, you do that very skillfully!" he admired.

"Well, just you remember. I'm very handy with a knife. Chop, chop! Never temp me to show you how skilled I am."

She laughed, giving his body a mockingly detailed once over.

"I'll be very careful about that," he said, sliding up to her. "You're a nice girl. Remember?"

"And very, very good, remember, as you said?" They

74

kissed one another for a brief moment, then returned all their attention to the food, making sure *not* to notice anything that might or might not be going on in the other room.

CHAPTER → 10

Once the other couple had disappeared, Gloria simply reached down and bluntly placed her hands along his inner thigh.

"Now...I'll show you...what I'm hungry for!" she murmured, aggressively clutching at him as their lips met.

The woman wasn't in any way about to be timid nor misunderstood. Her breasts surged against him, amazingly soft and firm under the dress. Her lips were parted as they met his, and without any pretense—she wanted no mixed messages.

That first kiss was something that effected every cell in Denton's body. From his guts upwards. It created a fiery heated dizziness in his head.

Her lips were trembling, open silk; warm, moist and eager. Her hands glided up along his chest, arms then slipped around his neck, drawing her body even tighter against him. It was an out and out invitation to take all of her at once. After that first kiss he wasn't in any condition to care about stopping.

She sighed in his ear, brushing the lobe with her moist lips. "Isn't there...someplace...private?"

He felt the gentle dig of her teeth into his ear lobe.

He didn't need any encouragement. She might be cheap and somewhat annoying, and certainly not anything like Judy nor the rather interesting woman Bass had brought along, but she had one hell a way with her body.

He had thought that Gloria was pretty sexy when he'd seen her in his office that afternoon. When he saw the woman in her own apartment she was even more than sexy. She was sex itself. Even if it was nothing but a perfected act,

76

it was delicious.

The woman had greeted him at the door with a very natural, quite softly inviting kiss on the lips that spun his head with a dizzy sense of desire.

"Hello," she murmured, taking his hand. "I've really looked forward to tonight!"

Her dress looked like it was painted on. Her breasts pushed outwards like bulging ball's of supple ice cream; except they weren't chilly cold—they were warm and supple, and very well pushed up and together in a fashion of open display. They invited a man's eyes. The way her mouth moved when she spoke accented every sexual line in her body. Her lips seemed to be connected to her major nerve centers and each word caused things to happen. With every step she took, the creamy sea of flesh which floated on the top of her strapless neckline did a little quivering all its own.

Her lips smiled and her eyes sparkled.

It was sex; raw and blunt. It was what he needed after the hard day at work. It was what he needed to forget Judy Grant for a little longer.

The walk out to the car, where Bass and his lady friend Connie waited, had been a symphony of gentle hips and thigh touching, accented by occasional hand squeezing. She was just about the most directly affectionate woman he had met in a long time. She wasn't playing around. She had offered herself for only one purpose. She had made the first play for only one reason. She had just one idea and desire displayed with her every action. "Take me, I'm yours!"

As they sat in the back seat, she lay her hand on his leg and leaned close against him. Words weren't necessary because she wasn't the type to need them. You didn't carry on a conversation with this kind of woman; you took her to bed. That was it.

So, when she kissed him at the bar after the first few drinks and suggested that they find some place more private, he didn't need any second invitation.

Gene and his girl had already busied themselves with other things; and if he knew Gene, that man would take care to keep them moving slow enough to give Denton and Gloria time for their before dinner quickie. And that's all he cared about. They'd have plenty of time.

The moment the two of them started across the room, Gloria began letting her hips slid against Peter, and he could feel the delightful pressure of her thighs as they made each step seem like a sensual caress. Her hand on his arm was squeezing and clawing.

Then finally they made it across to the small bedroom. Denton knew the place well and the set-up was perfect.

Even condoms were supplied on the bed stand.

She noted with a delighted giggle. "His, yours or mine?" she inquired, picking up the small little container. "Hey, he's got a fancy one here!"

"Best to be classy while being safe!"

"Best being safe, period. In this business things would go down hill fast. I've known a few unlucky ones!" she offered, suddenly quite serious.

That side of her surprised Denton. Not being smart about safe sex, but that she shifted so suddenly from the very hot, seductive erotic to bare-bones business.

She said: "Hope you don't mine playing it safe."

"No other way!"

"Some men ... hate it!" she said with a quick smile. "But they either do it right or it's a no-no!" She winked at him, adding: "Of course, not that there's all that many."

"Of course. Every man totally ignores that great bod you have hidden under your dress."

"No. Quite frankly they all want it. Well, the men, that is, who want women. But I don't hand out favors for nothing. I'm not some cheap whore." Then as she reached around her back said, "Not cheap. Just fun with the right guy. And fully charged. And totally experienced in the enjoyment of the physical activities that keep a man and woman in good shape. I do have a good shape, don't I?

He grinned as she took a pose that pulled back her shoulders, displaying her breasts to their fullest. "Men like them. Always have. And they're real, hon. All mine. Always was large, even as a teenager. Boys always wanted to feel them up and down. And around."

She laughed at that, very carefully watching his reaction to the words. "But boys are boys. And they might have a lot of the hormones, but not the skill. I always enjoyed a mature, strong and experienced man...like you. I've always been really rather picky. Keep my body in good shape for the right partners. Can't be too careful, can I? Right?"

"Right."

"Like what you see? Most men do. I have more bounce to the ounce, and funnzie twins here are all yours to just enjoy to their fullest, dearie!"

For some reason the tone of her voice with filled with amusement, and she didn't make any attempt to hide the fact it wasn't important want he believed. It was all in the game. But, at least, the woman had a sense of humor about it—and all the conversation was teasing him to the limits.

She laughed again, very throatily and reached around her back and unclasped the tight dress. "Why don't you help me, lov?" she sighed, struggling and wiggling. "I can't wait until your hands are all over me. Do what you will, I'm your sex slave!"

She really laughed very throatily to that, wiggling with anticipation.

He moved close and after letting his hands prove that her breasts were very much the real thing he slowly pulled the dress off them, and as it fell in a ring about her waist she turned and arched close, letting her hips fuse to his with a little instant wiggle. Her breasts were very large against him, firm, full supple cushions.

"Think I'll do?" she murmured in a low whisper as their lips met. Her teeth pressed hard and painfully at his lips.

A rich, low sigh of pleasure came from Gloria as she worked her body against his. The rapid action of her tongue fed into his mouth so greedily that he was immediately aching all over.

The woman was fully aware of her effect on him and without so much as a word reached down and lifted her skirt, revealing nothing under it but naked flesh.

"Don't...go too crazy!" she murmured, grabbing at him. "Let me...first!"

He felt the condom slipped skillfully in place, as she

admired him with her eyes. "Now, we're ready."

After that no real words passed between them. Only their bodies communicated in savage thrusts in a mad need that drove them rapidly to a swift climax. He hadn't even touched her breasts until it was finished. Only then did he realize he was smothered against them.

"Darling," she sighed, "that was...so good!"

He sat up, a bit dazed.

The woman was already standing and began to rearrange her dress about that lush body. "I think we should join the others before they miss us for dinner."

Denton felt as if he wanted to spend more time with Gloria, right in this room and from the expression on her face she was all but reading his thoughts. "Lov, I'll share it with you again...promise!"

She took his hand, placed it on her now clothed breast. "They already hurt for you!"

Somehow it was difficult to tell if she was reading from some memorized stripped scene or playing him for a silly fool, or actually meaning exactly what she said. The last he doubted.

Then Gloria said: "You're a wonder!"

That sounded quite impulsive and honest. And she couldn't be that good an actor.

"Come, big boy ... hardly a boy, now, are you...let's join the others for a fueling so I can get a refill..."

His face must have looked puzzled for she added, "Of you, of course. You're the main course, of course. A horse!"

The woman laughed at that. "Right from the Wizard of Oz. I think. A horse of a different color. Something like that. Never mind, anyway. I'll be your desert, promise!"

With that they left the room, hand in hand.

CHAPTER→0 0

It was funny the way the evening had worked out for Connie and Eugene Bass. First there was the fixing of the meal. They took their time starting things, knowing exactly what was going on with the other couple. They didn't say anything about it and for some reason she got the idea that Bass was somewhat embarrassed.

And that seemed a bit strange, because there had been no bones made about why they had come here. In fact, she almost wished that she was locked in the embrace of Bass' arms. Yet, strangely enough, she was slightly happy that he hadn't made a pass. In a way that showed he didn't consider her cheap and "easy" like Gloria woman He seemed to hold, for no real logical reason, some kind of respect for Connie. And that made her feel really good inside.

Later, when the other two joined them for dinner it was slightly stilted and heavy. She found it rather annoying to watch the other two. The man ignored her, and she couldn't keep her eyes off him. Mixed thoughts plagued Connie as she watched Peter Denton. This was the kind of guy, with connections, who could do amazing things for a woman like her. And it made her feel cheap wondering what it might be like with him. At first she wasn't quite aware of what that idea and thought meant, then with a flush she realized exactly. That one stare they'd shared earlier had made her almost weak all over. She found him quite hot, and would have melted into his arms if he were paying as much attention to her as he did to this Gloria. Whatever had happened between the two had locked his attention like glue to the little tramp.

After dinner, the lights were dropped even lower and

they all sat around in the living room, a roaring fire high-lighting everybody's features with a silvery flicker. Music was still playing, but it was soft and far away sounding. They had all had a couple of drinks and were working on their third or fourth. The conversation was awkwardly incomplete. It fizzled out finally, as if everybody thought and realized that the others just didn't want to talk to each other.

Bass sat with his arm around Connie. No pass had been made. No attempts to even hold her hand. It was as if the man thought of her as "untouchable." Yet, that wasn't true; and they both knew it,

Gloria and Denton just sat in the darkness, a little away from them, petting, caressing, and kissing. And drinking.

She thought that the evening would never end. Then finally Eugene Bass stood and suggested that they call it off. "Tomorrow's a big day—even if it is Saturday. And I have a lot of things to do..."

Everybody knew he was lying. But it didn't matter much. That was actually the trouble. Nothing mattered to any of them. The evening had, for some reason, bombed and Bass was being smart enough to simply bring things along to a closing point. Better to return home that try to make the weekend work.

Nobody said anything against the idea and in a few minutes they were on their way to town.

Bass dropped Denton at his own apartment first—with his girl Gloria, who seemed determined to stay attached to him like glue.

Connie heard her say in a stage whisper as the car door closed behind her: "Desert time, Mr. Denton! Now you get all the trimmings!"

The moment the two of them were alone, Bass turned to Connie, an expression of regret shadowing his features. "I'm sorry about tonight."

She just shrugged and looked downwards.

"I mean it. This afternoon I had other ideas. I don't know. It seemed like—well, it was that Gloria woman. A bit too much."

Connie nodded. Somehow it seemed difficult for her

to believe that Bass was really all that shocked. It was obvious the man had the beach house set up for that kind of weekend party. But for some reason he seemed to feel the necessity to rationalize all that away.

"Some women," he offered, nervously, "are like that. You know. A lot, in fact. Just throwing themselves at any man within reach. Maybe too many. Some times the mix is all wrong, like tonight. And then…well, I don't like mixing class with…that type. You're something else."

She shrugged that off with a quick smile, said: "Well, Gloria was all over him, wasn't she?"

"Gloria the whoria!" he chuckled at that, reminding her of the pun she'd offered up earlier in the evening.

"Oh that was horrid of me!" But Connie laughed, even while embarrassed.

"Don't ever apologize for your quick witted humor!"

"Dirty-minded, you mean! Nasty…cutting…somewhat catty, too, too boot!" She was desperately trying to get out of the trap her mouth had snapped around her.

"A smart, intelligent woman can laugh at herself and the world around her."

That caught Connie off guard. And she suddenly blurted: "You know…I always used to be able to laugh at things…here in this town I've gotten so serious about the business."

"It's a serious business."

"Sure. But you're the first guy I felt comfortable enough to be…more relaxed with, I suppose."

"I take that as a compliment."

"Well, it is nice to let myself go! I've been so uptight these last few months. Trying so hard to get a break. And nobody wants to give it to a girl who just has raw talent and no connections or…quite frankly, the kind of experience they consider valid."

"Don't get sucked into that, Connie. It is all a game, and they all play it one way or the other. Sure, experience counts. And credits. And all that. And connections. But in the long run it is a matter of PR and a bit of skillful direction and film editing. Many a star has been made not from acting ability but how they appear on film and what other artists can do to make them look good. From script writer to film editor. It is all illusion."

He considered her features. "You have a good face. A good classy one. And that's important. Don't let people discourage you. Don't give up. With the right connection you'll get your break. In fact…well, never mind that. I don't like making any promises I can't keep. I will, though, see if I can talk to a few right guys or ladies who might be of help."

She felt embarrassed, really naked and exposed in a new way. "You don't have to do that."

"Don't kid a kidder. I know nobody does anything in this town without second, third and ten thousand other reasons. I'm not Mr. Super Duper guy that the women just fall all over in their overwhelming need to worship…well, I'm not a damn fool. I know the score. And quite frankly I'm as mean-spirited as that Gloria-Whoria with Denton tonight— on a different level. I play the bloody game too. It is there to be played. A man would be a sucker to not make the most of it all. But…with you…it would be nice…"

"You are nice, really. I told you. You make me feel comfortable."

"Well, that's a start!" he admitted. "All this seriousness. Damn foolish all that. Doesn't get us anywhere at all, does it?"

Bass started up the car and then headed toward her apartment. "Wasn't much of an evening, was it?"

She didn't really know what to say about that. It hadn't been much of anything. Yet, in a way, it had been something even better than their other dates. Or what Eugene had actually planned for tonight; and what she had fully expected.

"No," she told him in a small voice, "I think the evening was rather nice. I liked what you just said to me. It was honest and really…nice. Real nice!"

She leaned closer to him. As he placed an arm around her she felt a sudden comfort she hadn't experienced for months.

When they arrived at her place, he parked the car. Hardly had the keys been pulled from the ignition than Connie turned toward Bass, her arms circling around his neck.

They kissed, passionately. And she floated in the salty sea of that contented joy, thrilling at the delightful taste of his lips, and the searching caress of his hands against her breasts.

No invitation was needed. Her apartment was waiting.

She hardly had the door closed behind her before she ran for the bed room. Then a moment later he was pressed hard against her and she thrilled to the demanding speed of his hands.

She heard her own voice crying into the night "Oh, Gene…"

CHAPTER→❶❷

Peter Denton didn't think much about Gloria for the next few days. In fact he was too busy to even give much thought to any woman—*even* Judy Grant. All he knew was that Judy had been given her screen test. Beyond that he just hadn't had time to find out anything else.

It seemed to him that everything was exploding all around him, Production at the Palmer movie was on its way, even though the Big Star wouldn't start work for another week, things were getting pretty heated. First the cameraman couldn't get along with the director. Then the director was demanding more script changes. He would get one problem fixed and then something else would go wrong. It was as if the movie were jinxed from the start. Nothing wanted to run smoothly. He felt like he was sitting on top of a volcano that was about to erupt!

The evening with Gloria was the last moment at peace he had.

The woman was boldly aggressive, one move leading directly to the next in such a smooth manner that he hardly knew when or how they ended up in the bedroom.

"Well, now, Hon, what's on?" she murmured in a low sultry voice. "And what's off?"

The dress that had been hugging her body so tightly all evening now slowly slipped down and fell in a circle around her feet.

"Surprise and surprise!" she whispered huskily, slowly gliding fingertips across her breasts. "Time to enjoy my twin peaks!"

It was almost satire!

He had just stood there looking in open admiration as

her hands slowly glided over glistening white flesh in a very bluntly inviting manner. Her eyes were smoldering as they gazed directly into his.

"I want a full course, don't you?" she offered very throatily, hips swaying back and forth as she moved forward. "Dessert time!"

Then suddenly she was in his arms.

Memory squeezed the next few hours into a series of kisses and naked caresses. He remembered her as one series of shivery squirms as soft moans and squeals of delight accented every new discovery of pleasure between them. She climbed greedily across his body searching hungrily. Then later she lay under him as they mated like savage beasts.

The next day he forgot all about her; and her big boobs and sexy, loving body. Denton forgot about the eager light in the woman's eyes when he promised to give her a call during the week. He forgot to call her. The reasons: Van Horn was beginning to "blow his cork"—again, as usual.

Alice Palmer—naturally!

But she wasn't his only trouble. In fact she was just one large headache in an endless serious of headaches. No sooner would she be calmed down than Victor Bolton was making a big noise about the changes which were being demanded of him at every turn.

Between Bolton and Alice Palmer, Denton's life was made into a churning hell.

Still, things started shifting into some semblance of order. There weren't any more threatening notes. That was one big break. The Big Star had finally calmed down about the unglamorous clothing she was being forced to wear for the sake of a realistic "arty" movie. Bolton was at last talked into a more relaxed status that accepted script changes without too much static. Of course, the extra bonus helped to tame his artistic temperament: a small one of a large check.

Between the headache problems he would let his mind drift to petty little, somewhat feisty and unpredictable Judy, wondering why she had become suddenly so distant—even if playing a hard-ball game to get him to push for her "big chance"! Some chance. He hadn't heard a word from her.

Then his thoughts would drift to Gloria La Sota, casually remembering how she'd been when they were together.

At such times he'd remember his mental note to contact her. She was a fantastic casting couch-toy.

It annoyed him to think of any woman in that manner. Yet that was exactly what Gloria was all about. She'd come on to him at the first meeting in this very office. And been a fantasy dream in bed.

She was quite amazing.

Looking back it now all seemed like some fantastic porno movie. A rather deliciously enjoyable one. Every man dreamed of a nympho who wanted nothing more than to fully satisfying her partner on his terms.

She was one hell of a woman and if she couldn't act, that'd be a damned shame! A lot of "Glorias" simply ended up doing hard-core flicks.

But he guessed that Gloria, while lacking nothing on the sexual level, was destined to get only bit parts for hot kicks on the casting couch.

He actually felt sorry about that conclusion, for she would be bounced around like a cute toy for the guys to play with, and after that either porno or the streets. It was a standard, sad story that too many women lived out. The smart ones would go home and find some nicely innocent, maybe even dumb, local guy to marry, never guessing what their beautiful wife had done in sin city.

It all blurred in his memory. But he decided to give her a call. She had been very clear about wanting to see him again

And Gloria La Sota was well worth a few encores.

He shook his thoughts away from Gloria, even while making a mental note to give her a call one of these days.

Best to think of other matters, he decided.

The film flashed through his mind, then ebbed away. No problem there, today.

He turned to the computer screen on his desk. He best make a note to call Gloria.

A few strokes on the keyboard and he found the file on Gloria La Sota. Betty had done her job putting the

88

woman's information right there at his finger tips. Name, Address, phone number, email, and screen credits.

That surprised him. He hadn't looked at any of the stuff her agent had left, only referring to the card she'd handed him in the office the day she'd been there. Now he took the time to see what kind of experience she actually claimed to have—outside of the bedroom skills.

He smiled at that thought as he saw a note Betty had added just under Gloria's bio:

Now, Pete, don't go crazy, but you're in for a HUGE surprise!

It was just above an amazing listing of credits which read:

> *Not only has Gloria made quite a name for herself, she is now producing films. She'd been highly successful, and wants to keep developing her career along more artistic lines.*

Then came a list of her most recent films starting with an impressive logo for:

> *LA SOTA PRODUCTIONS.*
> *Gloria has in the last year gone into private production of her own films, in order to make them ever better than anything she had been in before.*
> *ONE SUMMER FOR LOVE*
> *WHY I LOVE YOU THE MOST*
> *THE LOVE STARTS HERE*
> *NEVER SAY NO TO MY HEART*

This was followed with a rather long list of "Best Sellers" running over what must have been several pages when printed up.

The first titles were blatantly revealing:

> *YOU MAKE ME SO HOT*
> *SEX WITH SILVIA*

I'M SO CHICKEN LICKIN' HOT
RIDE 'EM COWGIRL!

Below the long list was some more promo copy:

> *Gloria La Sota has become an indus-*
> *try Super Star and has earned the respect of*
> *all her fellow actors. With her new company*
> *now releasing a totally different quality of*
> *film, she is destined to become the Top Porno*
> *Queen in the world.*

Denton sat there, stunned. It explained a lot. And certainly was impressive for what it was. He'd never been, knowingly, with a woman who had made these kinds of films. Well, certainly not one who was apparently as famous or successful and, as he'd discovered from personal experience, so skilled in the arts of love making.

Well, the arts of sex, anyway, he decided.

It certainly put a totally different slant on her. And on everything.

No wonder she'd been so firm and knowledgeable about safe sex and the use of condoms. Amazing. All of it.

In fact so amazing that he didn't want to think about any of it, at least for the moment. Maybe some other time. Maybe he'd find it really intriguing enjoying the woman for all she was worth. More than that, he simply had to ask her all kinds of questions concerning the making of porn films. What caused a woman to seek that out? Was it after trying to make it in legit films? Was it an off-shoot of failing to get past the casting couch? Or was it a different track, with rules all its own. He knew stories about many wannabees actors of both sexes ending up in making those kinds of films. It was a dead end, but could be a money maker. Sadly, many did it for free dope. Some prostitutes were nothing but kids who came to town, runaways, caught up in a desperate trap to survive, selling the only product and skills they believed marketable.

Gloria had not seemed anything but a hot lady playing the couch game for a chance at films. Now she was, quite

90

obviously, something totally different. And the more he thought about it, the more intriguing the woman seemed to appear in his mind.

Sometime this week he'd have to set something up with the woman.

He made a note to call her and then checked his email. Nothing new there, except a note from production about Judy Grant's test being set up and finished.

He wondered how it had turned out.

She hadn't called to say anything about the test. Strange. Normally a person in her position would have been thrilled and bending over backwards to at least offer a polite acknowledgement; especially considering how hard she'd pushed him. It didn't figure. Sure, the woman was a nut. Fun. But still temperamental; and hard to predict. The one thing he would have expected was a call thanking him for having arranged the screen test.

So much for Judy Grant!

Yet he wondered: *How'd it turn out?*

Probably okay. Hank was great at setting up such tests. As long as a girl had a figure and didn't look too bad on the screen, she could be given impressive "notices". Even if it led to nothing more than extra credits on the casting couch. It all ended up there!

In the case of Judy, if she had talent, he'd get her a walk on. If not in the Palmer flick, then elsewhere.

The next time he saw Vic he'd have to talk to the guy about writing something for Judy. He vaguely remembered that the man had pushed her into his arms, and had been suggestive about offering her a part in something.

Denton impulsively reached for the phone. Then, after an instant's thought, relaxed. It would be better to first see the test, then decide what had to be done about Judy.

Somebody at the studio had seen it. He'd find out.

He'd have Betty trace that down. Maybe he wouldn't even need to see the test.

But whoever had viewed the footage would have something on Denton. If Judy was any good, then there wasn't anything to worry about. If she stunk—he had better watch out!

His imagination suddenly conjured up a raging picture of Van Horn:

> *The man was screaming insanely, beating the top of his desk with a nervous shaking fist. "So—caught you in the act! Using company funds for just a few hot licks in bed. Well, Sweetheart, you're fired!"*
>
> *Then the features softened and took on a more sane expression.*
>
> *"Got ya scared there, big man?" the imagined Van Horn offered in a more playful mood. "You young Turks just can't jerk around enough desperate ladies, now can you. Don't you feel a little ashamed? Naughty, naughty. But then, we used to do the couch game in my time, too, come to think of it. In fact, that was a standard part of our salaries. Freebees offered for cheap promises of a contract. That was then. Dumb broads sucked up to us like they actually love it! Stupid. But they never learn, do they? Guess it's the same today, only a bit less obvious to the casual viewer. But, I suppose, plenty of those dumb broads trying to sleep their way into films. Didn't work then; doesn't now! And damn it, Pete, just because she pops a hot one at you doesn't give you the right to toss her a test. She's dead meat here. No contract. No deal. Nada. Got me, Sweetheart?"*

In Denton's mind the man continued muttering about the Hollywood he'd known as a young man, flaunting the delights of those past years when everybody wanted to be "in like Flynn"! In real life Denton had heard that story over and over again. Van Horn had a reputation have having mastered the casting couch routine, though in later years was less "famous" for such activities. He seemed more than happy to simply channel women to his executives and other help. Like he had done with Gloria La Sota.

92

The casting couch had become just a standard, normal reflection of what went on in every business, one way or the other. Dumb women thought they could sleep their way into a job; smart ones went to college, got their degrees, worked hard and fought the glass ceiling to break into top jobs. Even then, sometimes a woman had to pick her lovers in a smart way in order to open doors that would otherwise remain locked shut.

Shaking his head with annoyance, he smiled self-consciously. It was odd how one thought would lead into another. First you would start out thinking about something that really happened—and then you ended up with a distorted fantasy nightmare.

He needed some escape. Again Gloria's image flashed before his mind. He was truly intrigued by the fact that the woman was so big into porn. And apparently too smart to get into any danger health wise, as indicated by her insistence on safe sex.

Impulsively he put a call to her cell phone and was surprised to hear her rich voice answer:

"Hello, my love, what can I do for you that you can't do for yourself?"

He started speaking then realized it was a recording on her answering machine.

"Just leave your message and I'll hold it dear to my heart and return the call in a hot flash! When I beep, please beep me with your message!"

And that sounded down right suggestive! He noted with a smile.

When he heard the beep he said: "Peter Denton—"

"Oh, Pete, what a delight. I've been wondering when you'd call! Are we on for…when? Tonight? Tomorrow?"

The woman was monitoring her calls!

What a stunner, he decided. "Yes, how about tonight?"

CHAPTER → 0 ⑧

The minute Peter Denton stepped into Gloria's apartment he knew they would not be going out to dinner. In fact they wouldn't be going anywhere.

She was wearing nothing but a red see-through bra and next to nothing panties to match, with a filmy lace robe that was meant to hide nothing. She opened the door and simply glided back as he entered.

"Hope you don't mind!" she offered, arms wide at her side. "I figured, why play pre-games when we can go for broke? We both know why you called. We both know what I want. We both know how much fun it is being together. So…why waste any time fencing or being foolish. Like what you see?"

She turned prettily.

There was, strangely, something childlike mixed with that of a brazen call-girl. He couldn't think of her as a simple whore, prostitute, street walker, slut, whatever name men called such women. He didn't even like thinking of her even as just a common, ordinary starlet. Not that all those labels didn't fit. For Gloria La Sota was a porn queen, a woman who sold her tricks on film strips for fast cash under the table.

She noted the serious expression on his face. "What's wrong?"

"Nothing. Nothing at all. Simply that I saw your credits. Mind-blowing!"

She laughed at that, asking: "Does it bother you … me being a … well, porno Queen? Actually a best selling super star! I thought you already knew the other day."

"No, quite frankly. Just considered you..."

His voice faded.

"A fast trick and treat? A juicy loosie? A fun-'n'-games girl? A couch delight?"

"Actually…well, you were really sensational."

"I know."

"And modest, I note?" he smiled.

"No. Just realistic."

"Realistic or not, you're amazing."

"But…you're somewhat surprised at my fantastic line of credits? Right?" There was a cutting edge to her voice.

"I suppose." He felt uneasy, uncertain, wondering where the conversation was leading.

She was very serious sounding when saying: "Well, I'm the same woman, Pete, I was the other night. Loving, passionate, and experienced. I'm not a virgin and I enjoy being with a man. I haven't changed any.

"I want to get a break in legit films. And unlike a lot of the ladies who tread through your office, I have plenty of experience before the cameras. And I'm good. I know the camera angles, production, editing. Lighting. Makeup. I know how to play a scene and how to cooperate with the production crew, director, and cameraman. You name it."

She almost glared at him when saying, very harshly: "And don't look down the side of your nose about all that, either.

"Like they say about us gals, we all look the same in the dark! Right?

"Well, films are all the same in the cutting room. And shooting scenes are the same, no matter what the content. Some people are loved by the camera. As I am. And some just don't cut it. I do. I've made a big bundle, even after taxes."

She laughed at his surprise. "Oh, sure. I'm paid right up front, by check, via a very simple contract. I know the business. And I'm not a fool. So don't ever make the mistake of thinking I'm a stupid bimbo who doesn't know the score and how to play the odds to get the best deal possible."

The woman paused, studying his face. "Cold blooded as it sounds, I'm a business woman! I'm not your average chick bouncin' her boobies for false promises! I won't—and don't—demand a signed contract, nor empty promises, nor expect anything in advance like some cheap call-girl. I have a product to offer up and it is rich with promise, talent and skills hardly accessed as yet. I can promise you hard ..." She laughed suddenly at that. "Okay, I can promise you no problems and profits. I'm not temperamental. I hit my mark and say my lines and do what is necessary to shoot a scene in one take, if possible. And, between you and me, I'm all business! On that level, anyway!"

She sighed. Then a warm smile crossed her face, lighting those eyes with intense hot tease as they blatantly stripped over his body. "So there. That's off the table. Want a drink or something?"

Her short speech and brunt introduction had stunned him. The woman was far more sophisticated than he'd ever imagined. But still the Gloria La Sota he'd bedded at Eugene's beach house, and even in his place. And the way she let her eyes race down over him was enough to underscore that fact.

"Yeah, I could use it."

"Relax, take off your coat, unless you want me to make a big deal out of that."

"No no. I can handle the undressing, thank you."

"Oh, you'd be surprise how undressing can be fun."

She disappeared into the kitchen, then returned a few moments later. Obviously the drinks were already prepared. "They are strong enough to relax you but not strong enough to dull your manly powers. So to speak!"

After taking a sip, she moved close to him, saying, "Do you want to play now or just move in slow and easy?"

She laughed. "That's right out of a script. Surprise, surprise. I know a lot of lines like that. I have, by the way, a photographic memory. I can scan a script and never need to look twice. Don't be surprised if I run those kinds of lines past you from time to time. Gotta let you know I can act."

She laughed in such a delightful manner that everything she'd said before about business was washed into a distant background, smothered by the rich warmth of her nearness.

96

A shiver raced down his spine as she placed a finger tip on his cheek. "I can act wild and hot. Though it isn't *all* an act, of course."

She sat down, and urged him next to her on the sofa, placing her own drink on the coffee table in front of them. "Now, let's just enjoy one another, what do you say?"

"Wasn't that the idea?" he inquired, remembering what had motivated him to call her.

"Sure. Of course. You men can be so basic. Right?"

"Basic?"

"Well, a girl just offers up a bod for action and up pops the playful devil all red and fiery, ready to fork her royal. And the little...well, big demon, I suppose, doesn't really care how it gets cooled off, just so she cools him. Men are basic! Right?"

She was so light and cheerful about it that he had to laugh. "I guess your right."

"And many a lady needs to be convinced, chased after, gardened like a rich flower, given a lot of feeding and watering and pampering long before she even thinks of something more basic. So we are told."

"Apparently you aren't one of them," he noted, letting his eyes just flow over her. Or was it all an act. His ego wouldn't let him believe that.

"No. I suppose not. Never was. Not really. And my experience in these last few years have turned a normally responsible body heat into something which can be fired up at a mere suggestion. I think about it and I get hot. Now ain't that a shame?" She touched his shoulder. "You sure are a delightfully strong fella there."

"All the better to tame you, I suppose."

"Now, what script did you read that off?"

"Don't know." He found the exchange rather amusing.

"Try this, 'I can't get enough without you, babe!'"

"What?"

"Just try it. Just for kicks and hot licks."

"Oh. Okay. I can't get enough without you, babe."

"Oh, that was terrible. Horrid. If that's how you feel, you can just leave, right now." She stood, hands on hips. "I want a man who has real feelings for me. Somebody who will make me tingle all over. A man who has his…well, you know what I mean!"

He laughed, but she pointed to the door with a straight arm. "Out!"

For only a moment he actually believed she was serious.

"Oh, please, please, don't send me out in the woods without a hug and kiss. At the very least!" he chuckled.

"Say, that's *better*. Not *too* good, but certainly better." She sat down next to him, continued: "You'd be surprised at some of the lines you guys give a woman. And you'd be surprised how silly they sound."

"Oh? Really?"

"Really! And somebody like me doesn't need no darn encouragement other than a hot guy willing to play intimate games all through the night."

She stood, saying: "But. Business before pleasure, as they say in the sticks."

He stared at her for a long, stunned silence, expecting her hand to reach out for money.

"Oh, come here," she grinned, reaching out for him with both her arms. "I wanna be loved, with inspiration, I wanna be loved by you tonight. In fact, I'm yours for the taking. Just take me, you fool." She murmured those words as he came into her arms. "Let's dance!"

"Dance?"

"Sure, right into bed. I can't stand all this clothing! Mine or yours!"

Then while starting to dance him across the room, she said: "My, my, aren't you Mr. Super Duper! Man alive, I simply don't know what I'll do with all of that!"

As the entered the bedroom she added: "On the other hand, I'll think of something, Hon. Or is that Hun? You know, the Huns had no trouble in their conquest of Rome. Well, bring your hun into my rome…well, room, that is."

"My hun?" he chuckled.

"Well, what do you want me to call it? You're dangerous weapon which is used to simply beat other's into submission?"

"I'd hardly beat you."

"Well, how about just sheathing your weapon, please!" she suggested in such a low, evil sounding voice that it left nothing to his imagination as to what he was supposed to use as a sheath.

"Help me," she requested, taking his hands and placing them on her breasts. "Remove the bra. I never can do that very well."

That was a lie, for it almost disappeared without any effort on either of their parts. How her panties dissolved he never knew. After that it was a blur of caressing and kissing, stroking, literally feasting upon one another until nothing was left but sensation waving over him in enveloping fire. She knew exactly when to back off and when tontensify the connection.

He knew only when the curtain blanketed down over his consciousness; just a flickering flash of night. Then he was ebbing back to consciousness.

It was some time before he moved, and only then to turn. Slowly he opened his eyes.

"Are you alive?" Gloria's voice murmured softly. "I was worried that maybe you'd died."

"Hardly. But you're a killer deluxe!"

"Thank God you aren't dead...yet. I don't like to play Black Widow and have the man get devoured...too soon. I would rather savor him to the fullest."

"Lady, you ravish a man!"

"Isn't it nice that way?"

"It's amazing."

"Fantastic?"

"That, too."

"So were you."

"Thanks. Women seldom tell a man."

"I do. Think it is nice to hear, nice to say, and nice to see the expression of delight on the man's face."

He focused on the woman and found himself experiencing a mixture of reactions. She was skilled in making a man feel special. Yet he was aware that any woman with her experience in the porno business had the skill to create any illusion. How much of her was real? How much a down right lie?

But women faked it all the time. And men never knew for certain.

Well, not all the time, anyway.

"Like what we did?" she asked.

"I did. I don't know about you?"

"Oh. That. Believe me. I'm for real."

"Or one of the best actresses I've ever known."

"I don't fake it, if that's what you mean!

"Either that or you're a fantastic actress!" he chuckled.

"Oh, then I'm still in the city? Have a chance at the big time. Not just a quick thrill in the local flop house."

He laughed at that. She was rather fun. Regardless.

A lot of fun, kicks, and all that, but somehow it all seemed a dead end. He felt empty.

"What's wrong?" she asked, starting to gently touch him. "My, my, you do have a way with you, don't you?" she admired him with pleasure. Her fingers skillfully circled down his muscular abs, "what a man you are! Just what a woman like me enjoys to the fullest. So muscular and firm and...oh so hard!"

"Is that right out of one of your scripts?"

She smiled, knowingly. "Maybe. I really don't know. Sometimes...they are kinda ad-libbed, anyway. I'm pretty good at it. You should see one of them. I'll send you a DVD, if you like."

"Why bother looking when I have you here, and now?" was his own surprising retort.

"My, Peet-ter, you do have way with words, now don't you?" She leaned over and kissed him, very softly, and then ran those warm, velvet lips down over his chest, murmuring, "I just love playing these kinds of games, don't you?" She paused, looked up at him, winked. "Role playing can make sex so much more interesting. Don't you believe?"

"What kind of role are we playing, right now?"

"What do you want to play? Being my horse? I see you have one for me! I could ride it like a cowgirl. Just saddle myself and ride at full gallop."

She considered that with a frown, and before he

100

could answer, said: "Oh, no. I don't think so. You haven't been a bad enough boy to deserve that kind of treatment, now have you?"

He frowned, a little puzzled.

"Gitty-up! Whack whack. You know, how the cowboys whip their horses! Well, you could smack me around a little, not too hard, of course, I don't like really bad bad boys. Just slightly bad. Maybe a little…wicked. A little smack here and a little smack there can be rather…interesting, challenging, even…exciting."

"Another script?"

"I guess. I submit. I confess. I'm just one script after another! Can't help myself. See a man and all those scripts fall into place!" She shrugged. "A fall back, so to speak. If the man simply leaves me breathless I can simply let those lines flow out automatically, without thought. And you leave me breathless, pantin' hot and ready to fly high. So…I'm speechless with a man like you, my fantastic Hun!"

"Back to rome?"

"Well, back to the room. Or is it the Womb. Never sure. Terrible speller, you know! All the same, though, now isn't it?"

She smiled. "You're my six shooter! Or was it my saddle? Or horse? Oh, or was I the horse. I'm all so confused. You drive me out of my mind. Oh, yes. We were talking about whips and such! Smack, smacking!"

She had sat up and was leaning over him, her hands boldly illustrating where she might want to be "smacked" ever so softly. She patted her thighs, then patted his. "No S&M? If done right it can be deliciously wicked!"

"Never tried it!"

"Some men really get off on that, you know. Power games. They want to feel like they are big men with the woman. Strong. Or they want to be smacked around, submissive, after a…hard day's work at the office. Not that kind of hard, dearie! But…well, that's some men! And some women love being smacked around, too. For whatever reason. I've gone down some of those lanes, from time to time, but…quite frankly, I kinda like what we've been doing. On the other hand, it can be so much fun to do it all kinds of ways. You'll have to invite me to your office one afternoon so we can do a quick nooner."

"What's special about that?"

"Ever done it on your desk?"

"No. Sounds rather messy."

"Well, that's something that really can make me wild. Sitting on the edge, all glowing and with my skirt…"

Her eyes flowed over him, widening slightly as the words faded.

He watched her breasts swing out of site as she turned, lifted and slowly lowered. Moments later she was playing cowgirl riding a wild stallion at full gallop.

It was a riotous trip through narrow canyons, almost impossible to be squeeze into, then suddenly widening as she drove him furiously along, screaming in her delight. Her hands clawed at his shoulders as if afraid he might get away. It was as if she were guiding them around boulders and over bushes, across rivers. Then suddenly she froze, about to leap across an invisible huge chasm. He felt every muscle in her grow tense for a sudden racing charge designed to fly them right across the wide canyon to the other side in a one pow-erful leap.

They flew into space, clawing, clutching at one an-other, gasping in desperate madness, insanely locked to-gether in the final surge of driving force that landed them on the other side of some distant dimension which faded mo-mentarily back to the real world.

Then, after a resounding gasp, the woman fell for-ward across his exhausted body, shivering, moaning, "Oh…that…was…good….for… me!"

He could hardly think. And when thoughts did surge back into focus it was with a feeling of uncertain confusion. The woman had moved away, and was lying on her back next to him. When he sat up, her eyes opened slowly.

"Did that do it for you, honey?" she wondered. "Sure fixed me up right."

There was a cheapness to her comment, and a cheap-ness to her attitude that struck a wrong tone.

This lady was without question a dream-doll in spades. Lovely, openly erotic in every possible way. She was a sexual fantasy come true. No wonder she'd been such a hit in the porn films.

Yet that was the beginning and the end of it.

She was an ideal casting couch treat! Who could be better at that illusional experience?

He frowned. Wondering what he was doing in her place. Wondering if this was what life should be all about.

Now she wanted to get into legit movies.

Gloria asked, seriously: "What's wrong? That's the second time you're looked at me in that…well, judgmental manner. Does it bother you that I do this for money? I mean, have done the porn thing?"

"No."

"Well, I do want out of it. You understand. What're my chances. Think I rate a film?"

"Well, if not a film certainly a part here and there. If you can act any, I suppose you'll get what you're looking for."

"Sounds like you aren't offering," she noted, matter-of-factly.

"I don't know. Haven't had a chance to really think it out. You come at a guy so fast, like a steamroller in full blast. All a man can think of is what you're doing to him."

"Is that bad?"

"Not really."

"I can be very quite, too. If you'd like me that way. All submissive, romantic quiet and let you have your way with me." She reached out for him. "Even like an innocent little virgin girl."

But oddly enough Denton shook his head. "You've drained the well."

She laughed at that. "Reload and come back for some more!"

"Not tonight." He stood, suddenly wanting to get out of there and not knowing why. "But, I'll talk to a few people."

"Promise?" she asked, business-like, tossing her legs over the side of the bed and reaching out for him. Her face went against he chest before he could stop her. "I'd be ever so thankful. And you know what that means."

The swift shift from business to intimacy was unsettling. He didn't know what to believe to be real. Maybe none of it. All illusion like films.

She looked up at him, nipped on his chest. "I could make meal out you…an all-nighter."

All he wanted to do was get away.

But she giggled at that point, saying: "You certainly aren't fully empty…. Yet. Let mommy take care of it, you sweet baby."

Denton surprised himself by simply, firmly and even politely stepping back. "Enough, I have a very big day tomorrow. The star makes her entrance Monday and I'd best be in some kind of condition to handle whatever complications before that event happens."

"Well, okay with me. But you won't forget me?"

"Oh. Sure. Something has to be there for you."

"Even a walk on. I'd be ever so thankful. You know how good I am. Give me the chance and you'll be surprised. And you've only just had a couple of samples of little ol' Gloria's Gloria. I haven't even started offering up scripts of pleasure! I know more things than you can imagine. Even some of my stag stars were surprised on how talented I was. I'm famous…but really do want to go legit. Just don't forget me, Pete. I certainly won't forget you. That's a promise! I'm a hammer! I'm a pillow. I'm a vamp in heat. I'm…well, you can imagine how inventive I can be. There's nothing I wouldn't do to get into the majors! And I'm the best. You know that!"

He knew that any man looking for what she was offering would be more than delighted. But the idea of being thanked that much was just too generous an offer for him to consider at that moment. If ever.

All the way home he wondered why he hadn't stayed the night with Gloria. Nothing lacking in her astounding sex. Unless one wanted something more. And suddenly he wondered just what it was that he wanted more of. But certainly it was not Gloria or women like her.

Maybe just some good rest.

And so he had crashed hard and then come to the studio in a better mood, the sun shining and the world looking a bit more pleasant. Even this musing over what had happened the night before was almost pleasant, focusing more on the better half, than the more empty parts. Gloria was an entertaining evening. If nothing more.

And maybe she'd become famous on the casting couch circuit.

Maybe she deserved better. Maybe he should check around, see if there was something for her.

By the time he got to the studio he had once again forgotten her. And the days flashed by, at light speed, right through the weekend. He didn't stop working night and day. Everything had to be ready for Alice Palmer's first day of shooting.

CHAPTER ➜ **❶** ❹

For Connie, the week following the double date with Bass, Denton and his girl, was some what frustrating.

The evening with Denton and his blonde date had ended at her own apartment that same night. Bass wanted to make up for the earlier hours of the evening. He asked her out for that Sunday and also to visit the studio sets when they started the Palmer movie.

She never had a chance to say how pleased she was at the prospect of seeing a live movie set—let alone the chance to see a scene from an Alice Palmer picture being shot. They merely embraced and words weren't necessary. He was a nice, gentle lover. Fun to be with. Yet there was still no fiery electric connection for her. Just "nice" was the best word she could think of to fit her feelings about their love-making. She felt emotionally distant.

Gene was, realistically, a first serious stepping stone in a dreamed for career. How cold could she get? Yet she did care for him as a friend. A dear friend, actually. She was horrified that Bass might consider her just an easy casting couch trinket—nothing more.

This kind of thing was far too new for Connie.

For the next couple of days after that, Bass seemed to completely disappear out of he life. Except for a phone call which she made. After that she didn't hear from him until the next Wednesday, when he called to tell her that he was so busy that he couldn't see her until Sunday.

She would have to wait a bit longer to see him.

Waiting had become a pattern in her life; a standard which many of young struggling actors like herself suffered through.

106

Most of her time since first settling in Hollywood had been centered on acting classes, making contacts with people to advance her career; and trying to see agents who had already refused to give her the time of day. And avoiding, for the most part, the dreaded temp work offered when called by one of those agencies she had signed up with.

Walking through Hollywood, window shopping and dreaming were more enjoyable activities. Several times she had managed to afford a movie, but that was a luxury. Such film entertainment had to be offered on television.

Now her days had become a matter of waiting "by the phone" for some call. Cell phone or not, it was a torture of waiting. At least she could take that with her; not be locked to the apartment for fear of missing a call. Even an answering machine could miss an important connection. Of course, there had been the parties. But for the most part those were rather dull events with men on the make for a quickie. She didn't like drinking herself drunk and didn't go for drugs of any kind. Yet contacts could be made at such parties, of course. She had met Gene Bass at one. Still, even these were not a continual social activity. In fact, much of her days were lonely.

Connie's days always drifted, sometimes rapidly, filled with too many things to do; mostly, though, in a slow paced torture of waiting.

Waiting for her cell phone to ring.

It was a painful kind of isolation, even with friendly connections. Those people not partnered up with somebody were simply out for a fast, casual, meaningless night of sex. They didn't have time for anything but their egocentric me, me, me careers. Nobody had time to get into serious involvements. It was all a matter of win, win, win! And survive. And the grab at the next major step up the ladder to success. Or, as in her case, getting at least a door or so opened.

Connie recognized that she was still letting herself believe in a vague, uncertain future. But her determination would not let her even consider failure. She couldn't give up. And much of her time was involved in socializing with people much like herself, and those already further down the line, like Judy.

She missed the companionship when she had roomed with the actress. But that was a short-term event. Having a roommate was nice, but not smart, so Judy claimed, for intimate evenings alone with a man.

So it went.

And when Eugene Bass called on Friday at the last moment, asking if she had the evening free, she was thrilled almost beyond words. He was offering not only that evening but the whole weekend. It would be so nice not to be all by herself, and to be with Gene. At last!

That actually surprised her.

"What did you have in mine?" she teased.

"Conversation, getting to know you better…the normal things people do when dating." The man actually made that sound somewhat serious. Even convincing.

That didn't fit at all. A great, smooth, well-practiced act, no doubt about that. Yet she had thought of him as somewhat shy, even if a man enjoying "the casting couch" game. Maybe he was so smooth in his act that she'd read him wrong.

On the other hand, he was nice.

"The beach house," he offered, almost hesitantly. "Just you and me—alone this time! If you aren't afraid of being alone with this admiring male beast of prey who can't get his mind off the wonders of this lady who just entered his life."

"Oh, come on, Gene, the one thing we have is honesty, I thought. No lines."

"Not a line at all. Some women hang in the corridors of this town begging to play the party game just in the hopes of what might be offered and—"

"What makes you think I'm any different?" she wondered, almost half to herself, hardly aware of having verbalized the thought.

"You are. Believe me!" was his quick, explosive retort.

Embarrassed she managed, "I'm different, for sure!"

That sounded more bitter than anything else, at least to her own ears, for it was filled with self damning.

"You are, so how about it?"

Now she felt both excited and a little irritated. Not that she minded going there with him—alone. In fact that was a rather inviting idea. That thought was a lovely surprised to her because she suddenly realized how much she missed his company.

"You still there?" his voice asked.

She nodded, pressing the cell closer to her cheek. "Sure...of course. Sorry, was just thinking."

"Well, how about it? Just you and me! A real romantic interlude designed for two."

Yes, she would be more than willing to go for the weekend with him, That would be nice! Really, really nice. Wonderful, in fact!

He would pick her up, they would have dinner together at some expensive restaurant, and then end up at the beach house.

She didn't even realize when the phone was dead. A few moments later she was standing looking at the far wall, holding the cell phone in midair. Slowly realization returned and she placed phone in her purse. She didn't have much time to get ready for the weekend date. She could hardly wait

Yet, annoyingly, her mind hesitated. Was there any way to make Gene consider her really special, above the other ladies who eagerly offered themselves for vague promises?

Something a woman had told her brought a jealous stab of annoyance. Nancy whatever, a singer at some nightclub, had candidly said: "It is almost impossible to avoid the casting couch. On one level or another, they get you. I'm just glad I had Disney Studios to protect me from those uncaring wolves. I might have had to take a different track to get this far!" It had stuck in her mind. There were some routes that let a woman avoid the casting couch if she was lucky. Connections. And right now Connie was limited to Bass. Everybody had to start somewhere. Could he actually turn out to be a nice guy? Somebody who would be protective of her.

What a fantastic idea! What a foolish little girl's fantasy.

Still, Eugene Bass seemed to have become her first possible break. If he really was in any way interested in her as a person it might open some doors.

In any case she was committed to the weekend, and that would simply have to be played out naturally on its own level. And she wouldn't be alone; and she would actually enjoy the man.

So she was using Bass like Judy was using Denton. What difference did it make?

Momentary memory of Peter Denton and the way he'd looked at her for the prolong shared mutual connection caused a startlingly quick sense of desire to run through her.

The man was a real casting couch player and what a hot guy he was. The idea of Bass having that kind of look and body and connections sent a charge though her that was electric. But, Gene wasn't that kind of man. Thank God! She wouldn't be able to think rationally if Peter Denton chased after her—that one stare, that one long probing eye contact had spun her right down to the core! It had made her weak all over.

Shaking her head, Connie pushed all thoughts of that man out of her mind. He was a very real, hard-core casting coucher and she wanted nothing to do with his kind of nasty play. Especially when she had a nice guy like Gene Bass willing to be with her. Who knew what might happen between them?

She decided to enjoy the weekend at the beach house on its own terms. They could stay there until Monday morning.

Then she could go to the studio with Gene. Just that alone was enough to explain the very real thrill that raced through her body.

* * * * * * *

Monday morning.

Denton woke to find a bright sun cheerfully looking down on a sleepy city. Blue clear sky showed to the edge of the world, and as high as a person could see. It was one of those mornings when nothing dared go wrong for fear of offending God.

After a breakfast he had time to think about the last couple of frantic days, during which so much had taken place.

Thing had become deceptively smooth by Friday; nothing went wrong. No problems on the set; nothing in production; in fact it was almost boring. So today he wasn't expecting any problems.

The movie was coming along fine.

Hopefully things would continue on the pleasant level. This would be the first official day of actual shooting. The first day that Alice Palmer would begin work on the picture.

He had been quite nervous about the possibility of personality clashes—which were normal on a set with a mixed bag of talented actors. Larry Hearts, the male lead, was a serious pro, and might have been a pain working with a Palmer princess whose main talent was her body rather than any special skills as an actor. Larry had been warned to swallow hard and cash his check. The man had shrugged off all concerns, saying: "I suppose we aren't playing Hamlet this year!" Luckily he had been totally professional and not temperamental. Dave Carson was never expected to be a problem, a character actor who had been around for years and would walk to his mark, say his lines and never blink. Only Zane Blake groused about being third banana in a second rate film with a "booby boob" like Alice to screw things up. He could be a problem. Or so it had seemed at the beginning. Strangely enough the director had managed to smooth out personality clashes in the rehearsal run-through.

So, it was Monday morning and things looked great!

On such a nice sunny day it became impossible to believe that anything would really be too hard to take—or too shocking.

But fate had other plans.

CHAPTER→15

The Studio was buzzing with activity when he arrived, and Peter Denton really didn't feel the heavy tension when he walked into his office. Nothing was said to him, nothing happened out of the ordinary. There wasn't anything that had to be done; it was just a feeling in the air which he easily ignored. It wasn't touching him yet!

The bright sunny day still set his inner mood to reflect its bright promise.

Betty, his secretary, was busy at her computer when he passed her. She only nodded hello, but said nothing. She was too snowed in with important work. A good employee and sharp as hell.

Not long ago she would have stopped anything to look up and smile—or come into his office for other things outside of work. Those were the days when he had been working for another studio and they were enjoying a casual affair. Just a little over a year before.

The first day Betty had come to work as a temp, she had been dressed in a tight skirt blouse that fit the form of her body perfectly—and she had a nicely trim body. And, most of all, an excellent resume.

The first week she had smiled up at him while taking dictation—and in some manner they had ended in each other's arms. He never really knew how it had happened. There hadn't been many overtures. She wanted the job full time and was more than willing to pay the price. In this case she seemed to think that her body was a good down payment. She proved to be right.

After that they had enjoyed one another for a while, then each drifted off to other people. He met somebody else

112

and she'd coupled with one of the other men at the studio and they had simply stopped any intimacy. Later, when she came to work for Calvin Van Horn she'd suggested Denton to the producer—and that was that.

Interestingly enough Betty had repaid him for her job by this very one he now had. And this was a Big Break into a great future. Van Horn had been a major element in launching a number of big named stars and giving people behind the scenes the much needed experience and credits to open even bigger doors. Failure here, at this level, could cripple a career, too. A lot depended on the success of the Alice Palmer film.

Betty and Denton were very good friends. Actually a good working team.

In his office he just simply leaned back in the chair and enjoyed the promise of a smooth day without too many troubles in the offering.

His mind was jarred out of that mood when Van Horn called.

"Where you been, Sweetheart? Get you're sweet ass over here! My office. Immediately!"

The conversation there ended with: "Go over to the set and see that things get adjusted to…this! Can't have them just hanging around. Just get this off my back! You're problem! Return here with Bass. Then we'll handle the rest of it."

And thus the headaches began Denton arrived at the sound stage where the first shoot for the Palmer film was supposed to take place.

The set was buzzing with activity. Everybody waiting for the moment when the Big Star made her appearance. Several rumors claimed she had already arrived. But there wasn't time to worry about Alice Palmer. Right now the electricians and the prop men were busily standing by doing nothing. The camera crew was beginning to line up the angles for the shots. The second cameraman, was standing back watching his helpers do a lot of nothing.

Lloyd, first cameraman was talking to the director, but the conversation was low and didn't carry very far. It was normal for a movie set: Activity that seemed to get no one any place.

"Hey, there—you with the light...bring it over here!" someone shouted.

Another voice cried: "Watch where you go, damn it!"

"Oh, when is Miss Palmer arriving?"

"For God's sake, get that line out of the way of the dolly shot!"

"Darlings, darlings!"

"Move a little to the right. No! Too far. Okay. that's good!"

"She's been, you know, and with...well, you can't .... Hey, get out of the way!"

"Where's the script girl?"

"Person, person."

"Girl, person, blow ol' man Horn's cork, where is...whoever it is?"

"The script girl?"

"No the gorilla ape! Of course!"

"Hey, where's the director. I have his coffee."

"Any donuts?"

"Over there. Just don't bump into anything."

"Crap!"

Production talk.

Confusion and excitement. The early morning activities of a production crew getting ready for the first day's shooting. Only it was almost noontime!

Peter Denton walked in and several people swarmed in his direction.

"Mr. Denton...about the sets..."

"Mr. Denton...watch out for that cable!"

"Sorry!" He stepped around a large light and walked over to the director. "Myron...Miss Palmer is going to be a little late..."

The heavy-set, anxious man just shrugged his shoulders. "What did you expect?"

"So, want to go ahead with Carver scene?"

"What the goddamned Hell!" the cameraman yelled, turning on Denton. "I just get a shot all lined up and now you want me to strike the whole thing? Why can't that bitch be like other people...?"

"If she was, she wouldn't be the Big Star!" Denton

114

told him, starting to move away, over toward the far end of the sound state, where Bass and a young woman were standing. All he noted about the woman was she appeared quite stunning. She looked vaguely familiar.

But didn't all of them seem pretty much alike?

For just a moment his eyes paused on her, then pulled away.

"Hi, Gene—can you come on over?" he called, mentally dismissing the woman. "Over here. Another problem!"

Bass excused himself and stepped up to him. "What now?"

"Take a look at this," Denton said, handing the man a slip of paper.

"Another one?"

Denton just nodded.

Bass read aloud. *"Stop production or the white flower of show-business dies. This picture is death!"*

The man glared at Denton, a frown of deep concern on his face. "Does Palmer know about this?"

"Nothing. It came to Van Horn. He blew the house off. Right now he wants to see us in his office. I just came from there."

Denton looked over at the woman Bass had been talking to. "Who's the broad?"

"Oh, the girl with us at the beach..."

"Oh, yes, of course." Denton nodded in her direction, suddenly remembering that rather warm and intimate moment they'd shared when their eyes had connected the other night. For the most part he had managed to avoid another such electric contact; letting Gloria dominate his attention.

"Connie? Remember? Brought her over to see how things are."

"Making points with the lady, right?"

Bass looked a bit embarrassed, annoyed and nervous. "Just thought she'd enjoy being here. Seemed like a nice thing to do."

Connie smiled back at them, waving.

Denton said; "We better get moving. The old man is having a fit."

"Cork blowing time," Bass laughed. "Be with you in

THE CASTING COUCHERS, BY CHARLES NUETZEL

a moment."

Denton was half way to Van Horn's office when the press agent finally caught up with him.

"What's the scoop?" the man asked.

"Not going to tell Miss Palmer anything about it. Just do what's necessary to make sure nothing bad happens—just in case the threat turns out to…"

"You mean you're beginning to take it seriously?"

"That's not it. The point is that we don't know for sure. Maybe we think that nothing will happen. Maybe we think that somebody is just making a big noise."

"A PR stunt?" Bass offered, then nodded, saying: "I wouldn't put it past her to set it up. Just for kicks, or the media attention or simply a way to knock up the profits."

"She's done that already!" Denton reminded him "So what happens if we find out too late there's some nut out to kill Alice Palmer for any of a number of reasons. Things like that have happened before. And I, for one, wouldn't want to take the chance that it was all bluff and no bite and then learn too late that…"

"Okay, so we…"

"Hold it," Denton told him, opening the door to Calvin Van Horn's private office. "Let's see what *he* has in mind."

"Hi there, Sweethearts!"

"Hello, boss…" Eugene Bass said, sitting down in one of the large leather chairs. "Now what?"

"Now what? Now what! That's your department! What you think I hired you for? Just press notices? Hell no! Get this headache off my back! That's why I hire men like you. See what I mean?" His arms flung themselves into the air, waving wildly, almost as if detached from his body. "Get it off my back"

Denton broke in. "How about more protection?"

"Protection-shemetion Who cares? I just don't have time to be bothered! If anything happens to Miss Palmer the whole lid will fly off everything. See what I mean, Sweetheart? See what I mean?

Denton nodded, looked at Bass and then returned his eyes in the direction of Van Horn, "I don't think that," was as far as he got.

"*Don't* think! Know!"

"Okay—I don't want to let Palmer know about this!"

"Just get it off my back—see? Get it off my back!"

Denton felt that ulcerous grind moving like a branding iron of pain. More headaches; pains and problems.

The phone rang. Van Horn reached for the receiver and started talking. His face turned slightly red and his arms began waving.

"Here...here, you take it!" he yelled at Denton, extending the phone in his direction.

"Hello," Denton said into the mouthpiece.

His stomach tightened into a hard cramp. After a long moment he placed the receiver on the hook and turned toward his boss. His face was deathly white. He didn't even notice that Van Horn was sitting in his large chair, behind his desk, looking blankly at the ceiling, his face drawn and set like a stone image.

CHAPTER→1 6

Connie had seen a lot of movies in her life. She had read many magazines and books about Hollywood and film making and the people behind the scenes. But she had never *really* known what it would be like until they arrived at the studio and walked into the huge sound stage in which the Palmer picture was going to be filmed that day.

What made it most fascinating was that Van Horn Productions, Ltd, Inc, Co, Movies, .com, whatever name it might currently be handing out on its cards, regardless of how up to date and twenty-first-century cool, the studio in which it was now functioning was rather dated, and centered in "old" Hollywood.

"On-the-cheap tools. But then, a bad artist always blames his tools!" Gene had laughed as they drove into the back lot of the small studio. He went on to explain that the Big Man had plenty of cash in his own bank accounts, and plenty of international investments, but was a penny pincher and a cheap, third rate producer with unlimited ego and enjoyed pushing people around by the neck. "The man is a raving blow hard—and even if small potatoes in the business he's a nice big step up from nowhere for a lot of people. He was well-known for grinding out major first run stink bombs that made big profits! But you'll find it interesting. You'll get a chance to see what your up against. And you might even find someone you know hanging around, or doing something or other. Just don't make unnecessary waves, look but don't touch." She had assured him she'd be a good little girl and mind her manners.

It was much larger than she had thought it would be; a gigantic cave of plaster, steel and sound proofing. The sets

118

that were built along the walls were small. Lights and cameras, cables and chairs were cluttering the floor all around the half-room sets. And lights scattered above in the very ceiling, it seemed.

"See that room there...the one with the bed?" Bass had pointed out, gently moving her in the right direction. "That's where we'll be shooting Miss Palmer's scene today."

She just opened her mouth to say something when Peter Denton walked in, calling Bass over to him.

"Wait a minute...I'll be right back," he said, joining the man. A few moments later he returned. "I'm sorry—problems. Business comes first. If anybody asks who you are, just tell them I brought you. Otherwise keep out of the way of the production crew and for heaven's sake don't stumble over any cables or lights..."

She nodded silently. A moment later she was alone and feeling strangely lost in all the activity that was buzzing around her. After a little while she began to get more excited and interested in what was going on.

A camera had been moved to another set and everybody was starting to get things ready for the filming of a scene. Carefully she walked across the large sound stage over to where a couple of actors were beginning to run through their lines before the camera. It was a dry run to get the camera angles right and the lighting set up.

The director was shouting orders and interrupting the two actors at every word they said.

"Hey, kid—that's not the way to do it—tip your hat more to the left. And you...old man-stop acting like your were reading lines."

"But I am..."

"You're being paid to *act*—not read. Now run through it from the top..."

"Sir," a voice shouted from high above. Connie looked up and saw a man adjusting a light, standing on a narrow wooden platform. "Can you get them to..."

The voice was drowned out by a shout of alarm. "What the hell—watch out you damn fool!"

Somebody stumbled over a cord and one of the large lights came crashing downwards, exploding into a shatter of glass.

"What you do that for?" the director demanded, turning on the helpless young man who had been unfortunate enough to have caused the accident.

"I didn't mean…"

"Oh, Christ! Can't you watch where you're going?"

"Sorry..."

"Wasn't his fault!"

"You telling me? Nobody's to blame but the Horn man, who's too cheap to run things in a modern way with computers and—if it is old he buys it on the cheap and stuffs it in here for us to use! To hell with it—somebody clean up the mess—fast! We have a big shooting schedule today!"

Connie felt sorry for the young man. She knew how it felt to do something a little stupid and then be made a fool of. But she didn't have much time to think about it, because just at that moment there was the sound of confusion from the far end of the stage.

Everybody turned.

It was Alice Palmer and her parade of aides.

"Well, Darlings, I'm here at last!" she shouted as if everybody had been breathlessly awaiting her arrival. Which in fact they had been, and for hours. "Just tell me where to set things up and away we go!"

She glided up to the director and her arms flew around his neck. After a quick peck on the cheek she moved to the cameraman and gave him an affectionate "stage" kiss.

"Well, Lloyd—you got things all ready..." her voice broke off, moving from the cameraman. She turned toward the set. "That's not the scene I was going to be doing." Then she glared at Myron, the director. "What's going on here! I'm not waiting around while a bunch of hacks work their parts out...I have too many other important things to do!"

"Like what, baby?" the director managed.

"Like screw you!" she snapped.

"My damned luck!"

"That'd be the day, darling! But then, I suppose you forgot we've been there, done that and…" Her voice drifted as she turned to see a man she knew. "Darling, do you have something for your sweetie?"

120

She flung her arms around his neck, and her body hugged rather aggressively against his. "You're a site for a sore bod!"

Gathering the man's arm in hers she called over her shoulder: "I'll be ready for my shot when you're ready for me!"

"Freeze it, Alice!" the director snapped. "Just you stay put! We don't need problems. Things have been working out just fine up until now. Let's not ruin things on the first day!"

The woman became a rigid statue, then slowly turned.

For the first time since Connie had come onto the set, there was a complete, dead silence.

Alice Palmer's eyes met those of the prime dictator of the set. "Myron, I can always be very nice to a lovely man like you, if you just ask nicely."

"This is business. And quite frankly, sweetie, we don't need you or anybody else playing hard ball with me or anybody else on the set. Learn your lines and stand on your mark, speak when told to, and we're get along just fine. Is that clear?"

"Oh, but what if I don't feel like it!"

"Then fake it nice, Darling! You know how to fake it, now, don't you?"

"Oh, my, my," she retorted, suddenly all sweetness. "I never have to. But I bet you men would fake it…if you could!"

That last was snapped coldly, hard-lined as her eyes slashed across his body like razor sharp knifes.

The silence was almost deadly, only broken by a distant muffled snicker.

Then Alice Palmer laughed, shrilly. "Oh, come on! Can't you guys take a joke?"

The air cracked, shattered and there were a few snickers and finally a burst of laughter.

Only the director was icily non-moving. As people began to notice a chill once again froze the air as all eyes moved to the rigid director.

"You might think that's funny, Miss Palmer! I

don't!" Myron stated, not even moving. "There can only be one Commander on the set. And, Darling, it ain't you!"

A very loud silence now ripped through the air. Alice Palmer just stood there with her mouth half open, then suddenly it snapped shut. She shrugged. Offered a quick smile, as if it didn't matter what the man said.

The silence continued, lingering. It had changed into a deadly tomb where even the evil spirits were afraid to tip-toe across their own graves.

Everybody waited for someone else to do something or say anything. Then finally Alice Palmer broke the hard quiet, in the regal manner of a Queen making some major statement to her court.

"I really don't see what's wrong! I'm famous for knowing my lines and delivering them letter perfect, every time. I've been a pro for a long time. After all, *I'm* the Star here, and don't you forget it! Little ol' director *mine!*"

"So?" Myron countered. "Be a Star! Show us what a real star and pro can be like in getting here on time and being cooperative and zip the lip!"

She reddened violently and then turned savagely and started across the stage. "I come here to work and what do I get? I don't have to take that from ..."

Her voice faded out.

There was a deep sigh. Then the tension broke—somebody snickered nervously.

The director looked around him, astonished. "Well, that's quite a woman for you!"

The tone of his words held the fullest of contempt. The word "bitch" was obviously his real meaning.

Somebody laughed and then others joined.

Connie didn't know what to think. For a long time she was completely confused. In one way she could see Alice Palmer's side of things. But then, she realized, that might have only been because she had been a fan of the actor.

"What're you doing here?" a voice demanded at her side.

She turned. It was the director.

Oh, my god! He's going to crush me up like an elephant stepping on an ant. Frantically she tried to compose

122

herself, gathering up every acting trick she'd ever learned. She gave out with her friendliest smile.

"Eugene Bass let me in ..."

The man nodded and then went on past her. He had forgotten all about the matter by the time he was a couple of feet away.

Nobody noticed her at all from then on.

Connie worried about when Bass would join her. She felt suddenly lost and lonely. Helpless among strangers.

* * * * * * *

Denton's first reaction, after hanging up the phone in Van Horn's office, was to go right through the ceiling. It seemed that one thing after another was happening to make things impossible. At this point he couldn't imagine the picture ever being completed. He couldn't even imagine this day ever getting finished.

"Now what?" he asked the air surrounding him.

"Now what, the man says!" shouted Van Horn, jerking upwards and pounding his fist on the desk. "That's what I pay you to take care of. To get it off my back! I have other things more important to take care of."

"She's coming here," Denton announced, taking a deep tired breath. "I couldn't make heads or tails out of the whole thing. Something about Lloyd...or Myron and that he doesn't want to work on another scene. I don't know..."

The door flying open interrupted his sentence.

Alice Palmer rushed in. Her face was dramatic with anger. "What the hell kind of cheap studio are you running?" she screamed at the top of her lungs. "What the—"

"Shut up!"

At first Denton didn't know who had spoken. The words were too explosive and commanding. Then he recognized the voice as Van Horn's.

Silence froze the room.

"Look, Sweetheart," Van Horn's now silky voice said, "we have a lot of work to be done. There are problems enough in putting out a movie—without making them worse.

You arrived late and I ordered another scene set up. If you want to be treated with respect befitting a star, then you had better learn how to act. A Big Name in lights means that you are professional. Professional means getting the job done—when and where you are supposed to..."

"I'll get the job done just the—"

"Please, dear—I'm talking!"

The iron frigidness of the words was now beginning to sink into Alice Palmer's mind, and she changed her attitude.

"Look, I'm running a production company. I have problems enough. I don't want any more! If you don't get here on time, then you'll just have to expect things don't work out exactly like you might want them to. Got me? Sweetheart!"

Myron barged in, slamming the door behind him.

"Please, Sweetheart—close the door softly!"

"This *woman*!"

"Look, maybe we can get this problem settled!"

Alice Palmer was sitting quite stiff, her face set and white. But she didn't make any attempt to say anything.

Denton felt that this was as good a time to get into the matter if there ever would be. "Can I suggest something?"

Van Horn's arms flung into the air. "By all means, Sweetheart. I wish to God you'd start earning your pay check—By all means get these people out of here. *All of them!* And start getting this damn picture on the road! I have other matters to worry about!"

Denton quickly said: "Look, can't I ask a small favor of *all* of you?"

His eyes caught those of Bass, and the man's expression was that of subtle humor.

One thing, he thought, *Gene will do his damndest to help me out.*

"This is an important movie, for all of us in this room. Millions of dollars will go down the drain if things don't start to smooth out a little."

"Well, Darling, it isn't my fault," Miss Palmer started to explain.

124

"Look, I don't care *whose* fault it is. There's a problem and we have to work it out. Just try to work together."

As all of them left Van Horn's office, he turned to the director. "How long will it take to shoot that scene you just set up?"

The other man thought for a long moment, running heavy fingers through his thin white hair. "Should only take about an hour or two. Maybe quicker. Not an important scene, and the two men working on it are real pros.

"Okay then—go get it done." Denton looked at Alice Palmer. "What do you have to do before you're ready for your bit?"

"Dressed, made up and the whole works, Darling."

"Okay—*that* should take you no more than an hour.

"You kidding?" she yelled.

"I'm not kidding. In one hour I want you out on that set."

"I don't have to take that kind of crap from—"

"Get moving!" he demanded, turning and walking away. Bass followed him down the hall. "That was a bummer! For a moment I though Miss Palmer was going to stomp on my cookie!"

"Wherever that's located!" the other man laughed, patting him on the shoulder.

"Well, wherever...regardless, every time I see her I'm ...torn between that lush body stimulant she radiates and the almost terrifying Prima Donna pain in the..."

"She makes all men wish they could have a whack at her! That's her charm. That's what the van man is paying her to do—make them want her more each day! She's a sex object sold on the screen to blatantly drive men wild with lust for her rather oversize charms, blown up to giant size on the screen, and every man in the audience is wanting to be smothered to death against any part of her yielding flesh—something like that, anyway, so I'm told to say in the promo copy handed out..."

"Well, hot chicken, potato or pain in the ass I think the next days will be hell!"

"But you did good with her. I think she was deeply impressed. Good work," the press agent chuckled under his breath. "Great show!"

"I only hope so—God, I hope so!"

CHAPTER→10

It was exactly an hour later that Alice Palmer returned to the set. This time she wasn't in the tight fitting slacks and sweater, but instead had on a dirty and torn frontier outfit. The moment she stepped onto the set she became another person.

Watching at the side-lines, Connie couldn't help but admire the other woman, temperament, artistic personality and childish attitudes left the second she stepped before the camera. It told a lot about the professional ability of Alice Palmer's acting talent.

"Okay, Darlings—I'm here," she said in a tired voice. "Are we ready to work?"

Everybody's attention was directed toward her, but strangely she didn't seem aware of it. She was an actor known throughout the profession and the world as being always on stage in personal life, but the movie magazines never said anything about her working hours. Connie could now see why she was in such great demand. She had always admired the woman on the screen, and now she was able to see why.

The cameraman, Lloyd, made a last minute check-up. It really wasn't necessary; they had been ready for Miss Palmer for fifteen minutes. A stand-in had made it possible to set up the lighting angle, but still the slow routine was repeated.

"Move that arc a little—not that one...yes . okay, just a little to bit more."

"Good!" he shouted once more, then stepped around toward the back of the camera.

"Crank it up a bit Eddy," he told his assistant.

"Too much. A hair down...okay—right."

He moved back and then turned to the director: "Okay, I don't know how I do it! Just genius!"

"Let's get rolling" Myron shouted. "Quiet on the set."

Another voice repeated the command.

Everything became hushed. Nobody even seemed to be breathing. "Slate it!"

A young man came running over with a wooden slate-board which named the scene and picture. He took the top part and slammed it downwards, in the old fashioned manner. Smack!

The camera was already moving.

Alice Palmer was just starting to open her mouth to speak her first lines, when it happened...

* * * * * * *

Peter Denton was in his own office when he heard the news. At first he couldn't believe it. The information left him stunned.

"God!" he shouted at the phone, after a long silence.

He didn't move. His face had become dead white, and his head felt like somebody had just placed a heavy blanket of ice over it. He wasn't even breathing for a full minute, then the demanding pain in his lungs sucked in an agonized breath of air.

"Good God, no!" he shouted, still unable to believe what he'd heard. "It can't be—God no!"

The voice at the other end of the line started explaining in detail, but Denton didn't hear. The only thing he was conscious of were those first four words. They were repeating in his mind:

Alice Palmer is dead!

Alice Palmer is dead...Alice Palmer is dead.

Finally he consciously forced control over his numbed mind and shouted into the phone: "I'll be right over!"

On the way to the set his brain was running madly in every direction at once. It seemed as if he were hearing three

128

different conversations at once.

What would Van Horn say? The picture was shot to hell! Where would they go from here? What a publicity boon this would be! Van Horn would blow his cork! Who the hell could have?... The damn fool that was responsible—he couldn't help feeling sorry for the guy...it would make a fortune for the picture—they'd have to get something else to...God, why? Why to him? The world would be shocked What would Van Horn say? Alice Palmer dead. Everybody knew that the letters had been crank...but she was dead now. They must have been the real thing.

Now what?

In the background Denton heard a siren. Then he was walking onto the set. Everything was in confusion. People running in every direction and not getting a thing done.

His mind was spinning like a rapid clicking machine now. It was as if, suddenly under the pressure of the blunt reality of Alice Palmer's death, somebody else had taken over his brain. This "outsider" had started it functioning in a saner, organized manner.

"Where's Myron?" he shouted at the first person he passed.

The man shrugged, rushing off.

Denton repeated the question to the next person he spotted.

"There" The man pointed toward the Palmer set. Denton rushed over. A second later he was standing at the directors' side. "What happened? How?"

Myron turned a strained face in Denton's direction. For a moment the man's eyes seemed to have difficulty focusing and recognizing who was speaking to him. Then slowly his features relaxed a little. "God—it was horrible," he said, turning zombie-like in Denton's direction.

"What happened?"

"One of those...those damn..." the man looked up at the ceiling where a narrow platform was spanning the top – of the set. "One of those lights fell ..."

Denton felt a sick nausea settle through his gut. For a moment he didn't know what to say. All he could think of was that some fool's head was going to be chopped off for this carelessness.

Van Horn's voice sounded softly to his left.

"How?" was the only word the producer used.

Denton turned. Never had he seen a man look more stunned. Van Horn's face had no expression on it at all. He looked like a ghost.

"I just got here myself."

"Did somebody call the police?"

Denton glanced at Myron. The director nodded.

"Anything we can do here?" the studio executive questioned in a low, flat-sounding voice.

"Nothing."

"Okay then! Peter, come along with me. Somebody get hold of Gene Bass! We have things to take care of—and fast!" He looked at the director. "You handle things here—then come to my office."

"The police should be here any moment—do you want me to tell the whole thing."

"Don't be an ass, Sweetheart. Don't play games with the cops. All we need is to get loused up with the police. Tell the whole story if you want—no! I want Bass to tell the story...Just answer their questions, and leave it at that!"

That ended the conversation; Van Horn turned, and after motioning Denton to follow him, started across the sound stage. A moment later they were walking through the studio lot and finally up the steps which led to the producer's private office.

Once they were alone, Van Horn faced Denton. His features were quite serious and he seemed to be having trouble controlling the angry fury from distorting their rugged lines completely out of recognizable shape. "Okay, have a seat. We have things to talk over."

Denton sat in the large chair opposite that of the other man. Just as Van Horn leaned forward in his seat to say something, the door burst open and Eugene Bass rushed in.

"What the hell happened?" the press agent demanded.

"Didn't they tell you?" Denton asked, turning in the man's direction.

"What?"

130

"Alice Palmer was just killed!"

Bass became a frozen, living statue.

"Come on, man! Snap out of it!" Van Horn demanded, waving Bass into one of the chairs that lined the wall. "We have things to take care of—and fast!"

It only took Bass a moment to recover and settle himself in the seat Van Horn had indicated.

"Okay, boys—here's the problem. What are we going to tell the news media?" Van Horn was leaning forward with his arms placed on the desk top. His face was tense and deathly serious. "There are several things that come off the top of my mind—but let's see what you two boys might have to offer!"

The change of attitude in Van Horn's personality was shocking, revealing of the true nature of the man. Both Denton and Bass had never seen him like this before. All the "Sweethearts" were gone, now. The sugar and false Hollywood front. He was all serious business.

"Well off the top of my head, so to speak," Bass started to say, "I think the best thing to do would be let the whole story get out. Maybe doctored up a little to make it even more interesting..."

"I thought of that!" Van Horn interrupted. "I hate using Miss Palmer's death as a publicity stunt. You have to remember the public isn't as dumb as we would like to believe. They can see through the damnedest things. If we played this down, it might help the picture...on the other hand, if we made the mistake of pushing it and the public got the wrong ideas about it..."

"See what you mean..."

Denton broke in for the first time. "What about playing it by ear. Answering the questions as they are asked. Not trying to get publicity. Let it come in its own way."

"It'll come, believe me," Bass assured him.

Van Horn nodded: "You can't really control the media, only do the right thing at the right time and try to look honest. Look what happened to Nixon! Bush—both of them. Even Ronnie. The best damned communicating machine to hit Washington. If these power masters can be ripping and shorting, bowing and scraping or ramming up against a stone wall, just because some friggin' jerk is sitting in front of a camera and getting his ego licks at playing with the facts … today everything is black and white. So we should be smart."

"Does that mean we tell them all?" Denton wanted to know. It was more a mental thought spoken out loud. But the question hit the core of their problem. "This will be big enough news without making it any more dramatic."

Bass was first to speak: "Damage control can be more damning and dangerous than simply letting things happen naturally. We aren't to blame here."

"Holding back the details of those letters," Van Horn noted, softly, "isn't going to help us."

"It all happened so fast. And just standard crank stuff we hardly noted, nor took seriously. And, after all, we did put into place the necessary protection, just in case."

"Yes, Gene. We did that. And that bitch used it all to bump up her contract. I figured it was all a play by somebody working for her. I wouldn't have put it past her. In fact, that's *exactly* what I believed. And that's how we play … played it!" The man's eyes narrowed, then widened as if inspired. "We figured it a contract ploy on her part and literally bought into it. Now didn't we do that, Sweetheart?"

"That's the lines I was thinking along," Bass quickly said, agreeing with the man's obvious decision.

Van Horn told the two of them. "Okay, then—*that's decided!*"

The man leaned back and studied them with narrowed eyes. "Now we have another problem."

There was a short silence after that statement. Denton thought he knew what was coming—and he didn't know if he really liked it.

"I believe, Sweethearts, that this is where the crap bounces on the floor! Splat right into our faces...well—we have a movie to make and bluntly put: who's going to replace Miss Palmer?"

The silence after that was awkward, as if nobody really wanted to admit that they were so cold-blooded that they thought the picture could be more important than a human life. It seemed like a bad time to be talking about such matters. Yet, Denton knew, it was a very important and prac-

132

tical thing. Big money was behind the Palmer movie and it would be necessary to have somebody to replace her with before the backers decided to pull out. It was merely damage control on a large scale.

"What about..." Bass' voice faded out momentarily then it picked up again. "Somebody new?"

Van Horn jerked upright. "You blown your cork? You crazy or something? We can't use somebody new. That's impossible. Oh, God! What kind of people do..."

"Wait a minute!" Denton cried, suddenly cutting off Van Horn's sentence. The producer looked angrily in his direction.

"Why *not* somebody new?" Denton continued, thinking about the possibility of getting Judy Grant a contract. "It might be a boon to the whole production. There must be hundreds of starlets who can do the job. It will make them stars overnight. What a..."

"What an idea!" Bass exploded into the conversation. "Look at it this way: Alice Palmer dies and leaves a vacant place in the hearts of the American public. Now, somebody has to replace—no, not replace, but rather step into the limelight—and so we get somebody new and young and different. The part isn't that difficult, and just think of all the ready-made publicity! Campaigns could be shoved at the public which would make the Presidential Elections look like child's play. Everybody will be shocked by the death of Alice Palmer. We play that down. But then comes the fact that she died making a movie for Calvin Van Horn. Who will replace her? And can *anybody* really replace the Alice Palmer? Whispering campaigns. Articles. Interviews. *Studio discovers a new talent!* Think of it! Any established star stepping into the role wouldn't mean a thing—but somebody new...this would make the death of Alice Palmer seem..."

"Like we were glad!" Van Horn finished sarcastically.

"No! Not at all, if it's handled right," Denton put in. "We can make her look like some kind of angel. Play up a little fiction. Make it look like Alice Palmer had always wanted to give young talent a chance. We might even create a new Academy Special Award: The Alice Palmer Award for the most outstanding new talent of the year."

Van Horn showed interest for the first time. His eye-brows raised slightly, arching in thought: "Maybe you have something there...The automatic focus on the film via the media coverage of Palmer's death is a natural, of course. Maybe if we can play it up right, or down right, or left of center, whatever that makes things work for us ...let me think about it for a second..."

All was quiet. Then suddenly the big man stood. His fist smashed loudly on the desk. "Okay, Sweethearts, I just got a great idea. Here's what we do." He was the false front Big Shot Van Horn once more. "We play the Palmer death as if it were a terrible, natural accident. Then we make this search for talent. Big campaign. Across the nation. All show—because in reality we'll just find someone here in town who can fill the bill. Anybody that looks good in front of the camera. Who cares if she can act or not. We can fix all that in the cutting room. If she has any talent, that's nice. Get the best list of possible ladies and decide—fast! From then on it'll be a natural. The machinery is already clicking away. Do it. We will create a new star in the heavens, riding on the tale of Alice Palmer's demise. And...quite frankly...maybe this is all a blessing. God bless her crappy soul. That Palmer woman was a cheap slut in heat and nothing but a pain in the ass. Never liked her, personally. But you all knew that. She was...is...yesterday's history. We have found a new star to light up the skies in her lovely wake. Of course, we'll bow our heads in pain over her tragic death. After all she was one special lady. Hell, to be truthful, my dear friends, Alice & old vanny boy enjoyed quite a horn blowing affair early on, before she got too big for her panties. In fact, I don't think she wore many of those, come to think of it. Did she Pete?"

"I wouldn't know."

"You wouldn't? I thought the two of you surely smacked a few quickies—oh, but of course, I suppose not enough time. The show hadn't really started and she gener-ally didn't make a play for anybody new until things were...well, never mind. You missed out on a great lady. Never better. They don't make woman like Alice Palmer. She was special and the perfect and ideal star for any producer to enjoy … in or out of bed. Well, that last part, you don't need to underscore, or even mention, unless somebody forces it out of you. Just make sure everybody believes we are very, very sad concerning her death and hope…well, you know how to handle things, Gene. And, Pete. Just find a new lady to replace her—and fast. Don't care who! And then we make a star out of her."

His eyes took on a dreamy look and his lips smiled. "That's a great idea I had. A real great idea. *The Alice Palmer Award*. In fact we can sponsor it...yes, a great idea! *The Alice Palmer Award!*"

Denton looked at Bass, whose eyes were directed toward him. They exchanged one of those helpless expressions. Both found it hard to keep from laughing.

That's Hollywood, Denton thought, as he stood outside the producer's office a few moments later, *suggest something to a guy and two seconds later it's his own idea!*

He shrugged, smiled at Bass and started toward his own office. He would have to get Betty to run down the footage on Judy Grant. If she had any talent at all, he would see to it she was the lucky winner of the search for new faces...

That he promised himself!

Plus maybe look into some other women, as a false front to make it look honest. Sure, why not Gloria? And who ever else that might pop up as a possible new find.

135

CHAPTER→①⑧

Connie still felt shaky as she stepped into the cocktail bar. She had needed a drink for some time but hadn't had any chance to do anything about it. The shock of Alice Palmer's death and having been an eyewitness to the terrible accident had been enough in itself. But there were all the reporters and police and studio people asking questions, demanding answers. All had wanted to know exactly what had taken place, and how it could have happened. And everybody's story was different.

Now, sitting beside Eugene Bass and Peter Denton in the dimly lighted cocktail lounge, she felt mostly tired and her nerves felt like they had been rubbed raw for hours with steel sandpaper.

"What'll you have?" Bass asked her as the waitress came up to their secluded booth.

"Anything good and strong!" she told him, leaning back and taking a deep breath. "God, do I need a good strong jolt!"

"Make mine a martini," Bass ordered, nervously leaning forward on the small cubic table. "Better make it a double—and the same for the lady." He looked over at Denton.

"Same."

All three of them looked like they had been pushed through a thin flexible straw that had squeezed their bodies all out of shape for a long agonized moment.

But this Denton really unnerved her.

The moment she and Bass had arrived at the office a sense of something undefined had instantly nagged her when Denton stared at her.

136

For a breathless moment her eyes met Denton's. The other evening when he was with that horrible little blonde tramp she hadn't thought much about him. But this time, now that he was alone, she noticed things that hadn't been so important before. His features were even and clean looking. It gave him almost a school-boy appearance. His mouth wasn't really full, but neither did he have thin lips. Just right, by her standards.

Bass' voice said: "You know each other..."

Denton smiled, a half-tired expression. "Hello."

From then on she'd been in a kind of daze.

Then the man said: "Mind if we leave you here ... with Betty. We'll only be a few minutes."

The two men disappeared into his office.

The woman sitting behind the desk smiled, then said: "Terrible what happened. You must be in a state of shock!"

Connie merely nodded and was thankful when the woman got busy doing things behind her computer.

At that point, Connie didn't want to talk, but rather try to sift through, sort out, what she'd experienced at the sound stage.

The afternoon had been hell. Connie was only able to guess what the other two had gone through—as for herself, she wouldn't ever want to see another day like this one.

Those last few hours still left her slightly numb and sick. She didn't want to remember, but her mind seemed to be in a state of complete short-circuit; it just repeated the same images and events and words and thoughts over and over and over until she wanted to scream.

Alice Palmer had just been ready to speak her first lines when suddenly without any warning a heavy light fell from the narrow platform above her head.

A popping crash sounded as it smashed into her body. That had been the last noise on the sound stage for several minutes.

Everything had frozen to deadly silence. Nobody could believe what they had seen. This didn't happen in real life—only in fiction.

"Is she okay?"

"Call a doctor!"

"Get the police!"

"No...see if she's okay!"

"Oh, God, she's not moving..."

They were only voices screaming over a buzzing sound that filled the air. Nothing seemed quite in focus.

"She's dead!"

"Get a doctor."

"Call security!"

"Close the set!"

"She's dead. Oh, God, what are we going to do?"

"Alice Palmer is dead!" That last was a murmur that kept repeating itself from different voices, some very close, others so distant that it was almost impossible to hear them.

Alice Palmer...she couldn't be—dead!

There was a universal inward gasp from those people standing there, it seemed to take place all at once, as if everybody were controlled by the same central nervous system.

The director was the first to say anything, and then all was confusion.

Connie couldn't remember exactly what happened next. Everybody was moving in different directions, shouting, saying nothing and getting nothing done. It seemed like an insane asylum had suddenly been turned loose on the stage.

She wasn't able to think right at first. The minute the accident took place her hand had gone to her mouth, muffling the scream of shocked horror. The scream had remained suspended in space and time—forever frozen from the world of reality.

She couldn't do anything but stand there, looking at the dead mass of what had once been the beautiful and famous Alice Palmer.

The background voices continued, but they became meaningless sounds.

How long she watched, not moving, she didn't know. She really couldn't see details. Just shadow in shadows, lights flashing, and sounds, sobs. And screaming instructions that were meaningless. But it must have been for quite a lengthy period of time, because the next thing she knew the police were there.

138

And things seemed suddenly more focused.

"Come on, lady, move back—please. We have things to..."

Another voice was shouting in the background. "Don't anybody leave. We'll want a detailed report from every eyewitness..."

She felt sick inside. For the first time her body was aware of the terrible ache which must have been grinding there ever since the careless accident had taken from the world such a lovely young woman in her thirties, her prime, and a great talent.

Somehow Connie managed to keep down the acidity sickness, and slowly through a thick, spinning fog of nausea she gained control of the retching convulsion of her stomach muscles.

The icy ache in her gut had begun to fade away and a hot flush seemed to work through her whole body. For a long time it was hard to keep from falling down into the hateful pit of black unconsciousness that was trying to fold over her mind like a horrid evil hand of fear. Her mind wanted to reject what it had seen—it didn't want the pain of believing what had taken place a moment before. Then slowly her will gained control over her senses and she started ebbing back to reality.

"You okay?" a voice asked her.

She turned and looked into the face of a young man. It took several seconds for her to realize that he was a reporter.

"Yes, I believe so, thanks," she told him in a slightly shaking voice.

"Did you see the accident'?" he asked, aiming his small hand tape-recorder towards her.

"The 'accident'?" she asked, not realizing what he was talking about at first. Her mind was still in a daze and it was hard to organize her thoughts. The moment she asked the question she felt foolish. "Oh, the...please forgive me..." her voice trailed off.

"I guess it was pretty shocking," he offered generously.

"Terrible. She didn't even get any warning. They

were just about to film a scene. No sooner had she opened her mouth to say something—oh it was terrible! *Horrible!"* Her voice broke off for a moment. It took several seconds for her to recover. "She must have died right away, though. That much is a blessing—I guess..."

She tried to smile, but it didn't do any good, because this wasn't the time to smile or be pleasant. She felt that it was the time to cry or scream or do anything but just stand there asking questions and answering questions.

"Could you tell me exactly how it happened? I mean—did you see anything outside of what you just told me?"

Connie shook her head. She wished he would go away and leave her alone. She didn't feel like talking about it; in fact she wanted to leave, go home and get some sleep— or maybe have a few drinks. But Gene Bass had brought her and there wasn't any way for her to get home without hiring a cab—and that cost money, which she didn't have too much to spare.

Sounds, voices, faded out and she was once again hardly aware of her surroundings. She felt herself being shoved backwards. Then she was aware of several people standing next to her—some were asking questions and others were giving detailed answers.

Her mind didn't really hear the words or even understand what they were talking about. Instead she was thinking about how Alice Palmer, famous Hollywood star had made her exit.

Famous. Beautiful. Still young; all the money and fame she could have ever wanted. And not even given a chance. One moment alive and breathing—just about to start using her great talent—and the next instant, without warning, struck dead!

How quickly the line between life and death could be marked out; and once a person was shoved across it that was it. Everybody else breathed, continued to experience living, but Alice Palmer had been smashed across that invisible wall and would never return again. No second chance; no final goodbye. Just wham and it was over!

So frail, life was. The woman's death illustrated that

point in such a horrible way.

It wasn't fair. Not fair at all. A person like Alice should have been given a chance—some warning. What fate could have done such a thing?

And they all lived in that place where death could wipe them out in an instant without notice. How sad that people wasted their lives waiting for things yet to come that simply would never arrive in time to be enjoyed and experienced. The moment of their living experience was lost in the desperate longing for something that never would embrace them. Death stopped all dreams, slammed shut all doors into the future, smashed every now to nothingness.

Where, Connie wondered, *would all her own silly little dreams of a future as a Big Star in Hollywood, famous all over the world, take her? Down a yellow brink road to sudden death? Well, everybody died, but not always before they had really lived their lives to the fullest.*

The next few hours were confusion and noise. She settled herself in a back corner of the sound stage where only few people managed to go. It was a long time before Gene Bass returned to look for her, and by then she was too tired to really care about anything.

"Hi, Connie—sorry to keep you waiting...but there's one hell of a lot of things that have to be taken care of."

"I imagine," she sighed in a tired voice.

"Want to come with me? Pete had I have to talk a bit. In a little while we'll run out for some coffee—better yet a drink. I could use one." He smiled nervously and directed her out of the building. A few minutes later they were in Denton's office.

Then they had come here to the cocktail lounge. And the effect of the martini worked very fast on her. And the need to escape the horrid events of the day became more important than letting them retread through her mind over and over. She paid full attention to the two men, and especially found herself being more and more drawn to the young producer. To be that close to him, with all his power, influence, and utterly overwhelming charm and animal appeal was almost like a drug. She wanted to reach out and touch him, be touched by him. She wanted ...more than she dared to admit to herself. So Connie just kept her mind focused on the man, instead of what had brought them all together in the small cocktail lounge.

* * * * * * *

Denton couldn't keep his eyes off Connie as he sat in there drinking his second martini. Everybody was too tired to say much; all three of them were just sitting looking at one another, downing their drinks like they were water.

His martini might have been liquid air for all the effect it had on his nervous system. The day had been exhausting. But there was this one attraction, sitting across from him, that almost made it worthwhile. He found himself literally charmed and fascinated by the woman's classic beauty. Her blonde hair flowed so naturally over such lovely shoulders. He actually felt guilty even giving into the almost erotic thoughts that she inspired.

Crap, she's only another pretty broad! Stop it! His mind raged angrily over that thought, but didn't believe a word of it. Some people meet and connect, instantly. It happened.

He might be in a state of shock. But with the cocktail and the amazing nearness of this woman between them, he didn't find it difficult to let his mind escape into a mental fantasy about her. But she was, after all, Gene's lady.

A lot had taken place in the last few hours. First he'd gotten the Judy Grant screen test run down, and after that he had arranged a showing of it for himself and Gene Bass.

There wasn't much to it; just a quickie love scene—a script that had been used many times for the same purpose. Some writer had written it especially for testing young hopefuls. It wasn't hard to do, but had been devised to reveal personality and acting ability. And, nastily, just how promising a young actress might be as a casting couch partner. Sneaky bastard who had devised that as a test!

"Well, what do you think?" Denton asked the press agent after the screen had gone blank.

Bass just shrugged.

"She has a certain amount of talent," Denton continued, after a moment's pause. "I don't see why we couldn't use her. After all, it doesn't take as much talent as it does promotion. We can always keep making retakes until each scene is perfect—the public will only know that there is a new screen personality. Just so it isn't too many retakes, cause that'll cost big bucks! Still…the public sees only what the editor decides is good. That's all they have to know."

Denton reached for the small phone on the stand in front of him. A few moments later he had the director on the phone. "Myron, can you come over to projection booth 3-A…I know the cops and press are all around—but we have other things to take care of. Van Horn is going to handle everything himself. We have to be more concerned with getting the Palmer movie underway. Right—come on over right away. See if you can have Vic Bolton come, too."

Denton realized that it was one hell of a time to be doing work on the movie—and trying to pick a new star. But business was business. And one thing he was thankful for was that there were other things he could be doing. The sooner he could forget about the horrible way Alice Palmer had been killed—or even that she was dead—the better he would feel about it. And that's what Van Horn had demanded of both him and Bass.

Myron, Lloyd, Vic Bolton and Denton had the film test run a couple times more.

They sat in the darkness for a long time after that.

"She's not bad, really," Myron announced. "But I don't know—is there such a hurry?"

"What do ya mean!" Vic Bolton's voice cried, half angry, half excited. "She's *great*. Better than Palmer ever was for the part. I never saw anybody who could be better."

"But she's an unknown!"

Denton broke in at that point. "Sure she's unknown —but that's what Van Horn wants. He's interested in taking advantage of this—'accident'…" Denton felt like a horrible fool; it sounded bad, but it was the truth. Van Horn was only interested in one thing—making money. And everybody could go to hell and back before he'd care about anything else. "He wants somebody fast so that the film's backers won't walk out. We have to have something to sell them—

143

and quick!"

"Where'd you dig her up?"

"Vic introduced us some months ago. We gave her a screen test a week ago—this is the first time I've gotten a chance to see it..."

There was a knowing chuckle and then a serious intake of breath.

The director said: "Tell you what. If Van Horn likes her, I'll play along with you! Okay?"

"Fine with me, Myron," Denton agreed, satisfied that most of the battle had been won.

"Great!" Vic Bolton exclaimed. "Believe me, you'll never regret it. I know we—I mean Judy and myself and you can work real well together. No more script headaches. The part is perfect for the girl ...and quite honestly, I always had her in mind, in my head, as a mental model...for the part."

Interesting, Denton thought, reaching for the phone again. "Fine. We'll try that out...see..."

He dialed Van Horn's number.

"Hello?" a voice asked from the received.

"Denton."

"Okay, Sweetheart, out with it!"

"Got a possible girl for the Palmer role."

"So quick?"

"Somebody we did a test on last week. Turns out to be real good. Unknown. Lloyd and Bolton think she might be okay. Bass is here, too—we've all agreed. Myron says he'll be willing to work with her—all depends on you. Want to see the test?"

"No, I'll take your word for it. Just make arrangements for her to see me tomorrow. Okay, I gotta get off the phone. Reporters all around."

The receiver went dead.

For a moment Denton didn't know whether to feel glad or depressed. It all seemed too easy. Much too easy. Things were working out just as if they had been planned. Something was wrong—and he couldn't figure out what it was. Then discounted that as imagination. And exhaustion.

"What the old man say?" Bass asked.

"She's in!"

144

"Great!" Bolton exclaimed. "Now I can get on with my business." The man stood and mumbled a goodbye and then left with the director.

"What now?" Bass asked, starting to stand.

"Right now I don't know. Have to arrange for Judy to see Van Horn tomorrow. The sooner the better. The main thing is to get things moving and the picture made before anybody gets cold feet. We don't want to lose all the money that has already been invested in the film."

"Look," Bass started to say, "I...oh, God! I forgot about Connie—Meet me at my office.

"Make that mine, Gene!"

A moment later the man was gone.

Denton sat looking at the blank screen for a long time, trying to figure out exactly what was bothering him. After a while he shook himself. That nagging feeling was probably only his emotional shock about Alice Palmer's death.

It wasn't that he had ever liked the Palmer woman. She had slept her way up to fame. But still he couldn't help feeling sorry for her. After all a life was a life—and Alice Palmer had been one thing: a pro. She had meant big box office. And that was even more important than being talented. In the motion picture business everything was rated on money and profit. It was true that you could sell the public almost anything if given enough time and money. But there was always that narrow margin where the unwashed millions couldn't be sold.

Alice Palmer had made the grade—and now she was dead.

And that was the brutal statement on the attitude of Hollywood. No sooner had she been killed than she just didn't exist anymore. Sure, her old pictures would be re-released and make plenty of money. DVDs would sell fast. Cable would exhaust itself digging up everything she'd been in. But as far as Calvin Van Horn Productions was concerned, Alice Palmer might as well never have existed or have been killed months before. The industry had to go on. The business of making pictures couldn't be stopped just because somebody met a violent death—accident or not.

That thought stopped him...Of course it had been an accident. What else could it be?

Yet, what about the notes? They had threatened that she would never live to make the picture. But he and everybody else knew that they had been crank. Now, Alice Palmer lay dead. It didn't make sense.

Slowly he had stood and walked out of the projection room.

And now this retake with Bass' lady of the day: Connie whatever her last name was. A stunning woman. Maybe she could act. He'd have to find out. He assumed she was seeking a career in films. Otherwise why bother with a nice, but rather unassuming and average looking guy like Eugene Bass? Cold as that was, it was, also, blunt and to the point. Women flocked to connected men. Bass was one of them. But Connie didn't appear, on the surface, as the kind of woman being bounced around the casting couch. He wondered. Then mentally dropped such concerned. This wasn't the time to be chalking up hot tricks for lonely nights. It would take time before the reaction of their second meeting would take effect—but then, after that, things would change like lightning had struck!

Even sitting this close to her in the booth, he could feel the amazing draw of her very presence. He couldn't keep his eyes off her.

146

CHAPTER→10

Connie had never believed in love at first sight, and it wasn't really until months later that she even gave the idea any thought. But in the cocktail lounge, so close to him, she was painfully aware of the Peter Denton in such a way that she felt shaky. At first she tried to ignore the feeling. She wanted to avoid his eyes. She tried not look in his direction any more than possible. But that was simply impossible. They were all sitting so close.

As the conversation started to pick up slowly after the third martini had been set down before them, it was impossible to ignore the man.

She kept her attention on Bass, when possible, but the sound of the other man's voice kept him mentally focused in her mind.

"I better call Judy," he said, getting his cell out. "All I have to do is forget *that*...and everything will be blown to hell. Van Horn will blow his cork and—" He had been dialing while he was talking; now he broke off, and the silence seemed long and heavy. "Hello, Judy?" he said in a silk voice. "Yeah, Peter. Have good news for you. And some sad news, too. First of all you have to come in and see Mr. Van Horn, tomorrow. Right. Early. Dress sharp, but classy. Be professional. Take my lead, if you want. Get your agent there with you, if you...okay, fine. Yes...the bad news. Turn on the television, you'll get it all there. Well...okay...Alice Palmer is dead and you're being considered as a replacement. But keep that quiet. Don't tell anybody. Gene? Yes, he's here. Sure."

The cell phone was handed to the other man.

Denton's eyes caught Connie's. "Guess all this is

rather strange to you."

"Rather."

"Well, sometimes things actually move rather fast. Right now, I would suggest you be hush, hush about what you just heard. There might even be something for you in all this...if you don't blow it."

She blinked, uncertain what he meant.

"Quite frankly, that's show-biz. As they say: the show must go on. Yes. Bloody cold. Horrid. I admit. That facts are facts. But for now, the studio wants to play it close. Gene told me you were a sweet lady who could be trusted to be smart. That's his take on you."

"Only sweet?"

"And intelligent enough to see how things are. Obviously the news is hitting the public now, instant replay, and live coverage! Can't be helped. But ..."

Bass broke in, handing the cell back to Denton: "Judy was blown away!"

"Anything left of her? Hate to think she's scattered all over the place!" Denton chuckled, winking at both of them at once. It was horrid humor, but appreciated by all three. They needed some release.

"That's horrid!" Connie found herself saying. "You two act as if this is a moment to celebrate, not..."

Bass gripped her hand. "Gallows humor. We're quite aware and feel a lot of things. But, bottom line is that we have a job to do and that's what we're doing. And...as for you, young lady, if you want a real start here in town, just be smart and grab what you can out of a nasty situation. You just happened to be at the right place at the right time with the right guy and..."

"Hey, don't I count?" Denton laughed a little sharply. "I'm the guy with real power here. And don't you two forget it!"

Bass shrugged, chuckling: "If you want the credit, take it. But...I suggested giving her a break!"

Connie was stunned, breathless. For a moment she simply couldn't believe her ears. Was this some kind of pay-off to keep her quiet, under control? But why? What kind of thing was really going on behind the scenes?

Denton, guessing her confusion said: "Nothing is exactly like it seems. All illusions and smoky mirrors, to be frank. Nasty as times. But…like Gene says: timing is all. In real estate is location, location, location. Here…well, connections pay off, and chanced meetings in the night or day or afternoon. And a lot of deals are made in cocktail lounges just like this—even on golf courses. Heaven forbid. But, right now, if you're really interested in trying your hand in this business, you have a prime chance. Nothing much. Probably a stand in or walk on or who knows. If you can act and look as good on film as you do right now, well, honey, this is your chance at a start."

Again Connie's eyes moved from one man to the other. Gene Bass squeezed her fingers. "Your first big break."

"And…" she almost said she was disgusted at how it was happening. But that sounded like a lie even in her own mind. The fact was that Alice Palmer was dead, nothing could be done about it.

Denton's voice cut through her thoughts, and their eyes met, locked, as he spoke: "How about it? Want a wild ride on a roller coaster to the heavens?"

The man made that sound like something other than what his eyes were communicating. The wild, hot flare of desire racing through her own body was reflected in his gaze. It seemed as if those words had a double meaning. And she flushed at the reality of that fact. He was making a pass at her!

Eugene Bass' fingers slowly released her as he said: "Sounds like we have something going here."

Somehow, Connie knew the man had done more than merely break a physical connection between them. He could hardly have not noticed the expression in Denton's eyes, and certainly her own face had been nakedly revealing.

Connie glanced at the PR man and silently thanked him for being such a lovely man, such a good friend, and wonderful sport about the whole thing.

Then she returned her gaze to Denton with a suddenly new sense of what might very well be right ahead of them. And who knew where that would lead?

Denton, still gazing directly into her eyes, said: "As much as I hate it, we should probably get back to the office...so to speak. I think it's gonna be a long night!"

Bass nodded.

Suddenly Connie felt lost. She wanted to reach out to Mr. Peter Denton and touch him, to make some kind of physical connection, so he wouldn't forget her—and some of the things they had all talked about. She desperately wanted a very real connection with the man.

She was about to say something, what, she would never know, but Peter Denton suddenly stood, saying: "We'll have to get together soon. Nice meeting you...Connie!"

The way he said her name was like a caress right down her spine. "It was nice."

"Yes. Very nice. I really look forward to seeing you again, soon!"

"Is tomorrow too soon? I could call you and check!"

That shocked her, shocked the two men and seemed to shock the whole world. It seemed the air turned to static in her ears.

Connie couldn't believe she had said that. It was mad, insane impulse. The cocktails, of course, were to blame.

Peter Denton smiled, and even though there was a tiredness in his eyes, the light behind that was very real, touching and quite pleased. "That would be nice."

Then suddenly the man left and Bass used his cell phone to call Security with for a car and driver to pick them up.

CHAPTER→20

All the way home from the studios in the studio car, with its built-in driver, Connie was somewhat confused. Her impulsive suggestion to call Denton had perhaps been foolish; yet have been done without thought. The PR man had told her, when she got into the car: "You're a lovely lady, just don't forget me, now that you're moving on."

"Oh, Gene…really," she had replied, not knowing what to say.

"Look, I've been around enough to see…what is there for you. And that phone call thing, think he kinda liked it. Bold. But classy. Otherwise he'd have nixed the whole idea, but fast. "

"You don't think it was too much, then?"

"Hardly. You have to play it how it is. Be yourself. That is special enough. He'll see that pretty fast. You don't have to be like the others. They are a penny a million. You're a gold coin. Very special."

"You make a lady feel that way, Gene."

"I'm not a fool," he laughed that off as the joke it was meant to be. "I know when I've been used and abused!"

"It wasn't that way, Gene."

"I think we both know that. And know what it is all about, too." Patting her cheek he added: "You're a neat lady. And don't forget that if you need me you have my number." He winked at that last word. "In spades, as they say!"

He then closed the door, and walked off towards Denton's office as the car started driving towards the studio exit.

Connie felt flushed and confused. The couple of martinis had created a glow, but more effective was the way Peter Denton had looked so probingly into her eyes. It was as if he were mentally stripping her naked. In a nice, gentlemanly way, yet, nonetheless, boldly assessing in a stark flattering way.

Her own reaction had been without question very hot.

She was also excited by what she had learned in the conversation with and between the two men. The tragic death of Alice Palmer had already been set aside for immediate issues concerning the film. That was their job. But how it tangled with her future was stunning. Breathtaking.

And July Grant. That was a real knock between the eyes.

Judy was being offered the Palmer role. She couldn't believe what she was hearing. It didn't seem possible. From complete unknown to Big Name Star. Abruptly she was happy—not only for Judy, but now for herself. There was little doubt that Judy would be able to help Connie, too. Any work would be heaven sent. Money would help. Maybe no more temp work.

Connie decided right then, in the booth with the two men, that if she wanted to get ahead in the world, it might be necessary to play down and dirty! Who knew what Mr. Peter Denton might have in mind for her; and what difference would it make in the long run. It wasn't that she found the man unattractive; in fact he had already reached in so deeply throughout her very core that it was unbelievable. Connie knew not to take him too seriously. But she could make a direct play for this young assistant producer. And enjoy whatever they might experience together. The casting couch game always set the rules for men like him. How she used them and the couch and the rules to win the right kind of favors would make all the difference in the world.

They wanted to make certain she was quiet about what she had learned this evening. And they were willing to give her a small part. A token bit that might open new doors.

But she'd have to play it smart. The idea would be to keep Peter Denton interested. Seduction was a natural act that drew a helpless man into a tangled female trap and locked him into all kinds of intrigues, even marriage—with or without a happy ending.

152

Marriage, of course, Connie realized, was hardly her target—and that's what she now considered him: a target to advance an acting career. That was her best, realistic attitude towards the man.

Her mind was a level headed adding machine, ringing up equations and the results in quick fashion.

If Peter Denton was interested, there was a good chance that more than a mere walk-on might be in the offering. Assuming the man played women to his own advantage, then it was only logical and fair to play him as only a smart, experienced woman could. Men were, bottom-line, pretty simple creatures and painfully easy to read when it came to sex. Like it or not, Connie had no doubt that men enjoyed her company, the seductive game was a natural outgrowth of just being alive. Using her body to get what she wanted might be the only device open to break down closed doors. She'd been a damned fool wasting her time all these months. Well. Maybe not. Everything she'd done had led to this point.

Now she had an introduction to a man who could really help her.

Now was the time to take advantage of her looks, brains and experience to seduce the right man. Mr. Peter Denton.

If men could play the casting couch game, so could she. Alice Palmer had done it with great success. The smart woman knew how to twist a male body around her fingers. Mr. Peter Denton might be a sharp, experienced player, but she was no stupid little innocent girl without a rather wide bag of tricks all her own. And, most of all, this man was obviously interested. Maybe even the kind of interest that went far beyond just a one time quickie on the couch.

This would not be mere seduction; it would be a down right hard ball dirty game between two serious players. That's what she kept telling herself. She'd be a tigress hunting her prey and Mr. Peter Denton was her first full course meal!

And, of course, Judy would certainly be rooting for her. That and Bass in the background as a fall back—bless his lovely nice-guy heart.

She had to become a calculating, cold-blooded machine aiming all of herself right at the very heart of this brand new, magnetically attractive target.

What the hell was wrong with her? she thought nervously. *What about Bass? Was she that frozen-hearted? What kind of passionate desire for success could make it so easy to plan on bed-jumping from one man to another?*

Yet, cold-blood as it sounded, that was the reality. Bass had freed her; Denton had already offered her a chance for a bit part, and it probably all hinged on how well the two of them could finalize the deal.

She didn't want to think about it anymore. For Peter Denton was her next Hollywood conquest!

Had she already leaped full swing onto the casting couch? Was it really all that easy to be sucked in, seduced right onto the couch for all to enjoy? Was she being turned into a studio play thing? Was this how it happened?

Connie fought with those questions and decided it didn't have to be that way.

"Pick the right guy!" she muttered. "And you're in."

The driver asked: "What? What did you say?"

Embarrassed, she shook her head. "Nothing, nothing at all."

"Did you want me to drop you off some place? Before going to your home?" he offered.

"No. Home will be fine!"

CHAPTER➔❷❶

The next morning Denton tried to figure out his reactions toward Connie Remington. They were mixed, that much he knew. She was different from the other women he had known.

He stopped there—he really didn't even know her.

Not yet!

But one thing Denton realized: it was just a matter of a couple of days—at most—before he would know Connie as much as any man could know any woman. Maybe even today; considering her promise to call him. Of course there probably wouldn't be any time for such pleasures. He'd worked almost all night with Bass. But if Connie offered a swift trick on the couch; why not? That was the name of the game. If a woman wanted to connect with a power broker in this—or any business for that matter—then she would figure her odds and accept the results: usually a quickie couch moment with bland promises of some kind of payoff, careerwise. Foolish little ladies tossing their bods out to be royally screwed by all.

Of course Connie sure was a classy little assy.

His mind toyed with her image in a half-dreamy state, before full consciousness opened his eyes. He was lying on the sofa where he'd slept in his office. The long session had lasted almost until 3AM and he'd been exhausted.

And he was a dirty, no good bastard! He thought, sitting up, head in hands.

But he was feeling annoyed, too.

Too many problems facing him today.

Slowly he stood and a half an hour later he had showered and freshened, shaved in the small bathroom off his executive office. Van Horn, at least, supplied a nice set-up for his top assistant.

All through the shower he hadn't been able to keep the image of Connie Remington out of his mind. What would it be like getting her in a shower with him. Was she as lovely stark naked as in that dress? He knew she'd be even more beautiful. The woman was stunning; a classic lady with so much going for her, so much intelligence and so much seductive beauty that it could make a man weak all over thinking of totally possessing her.

That imagine kept plaguing him more than he wanted it to. He tried to consider other matters. Business matters. And there was a lot to deal with.

He couldn't help wondering when Judy would be turning up at the studio, and if she would come to his office first. He hoped not. With women like Gloria hanging around in the background, willing to bring all that past experience in the porno-factories to the couch, why bother about other easy ladies? How he'd missed picking up on Gloria's very professional style and bag of tricks was something of a surprise. He was still a bit unnerved by his reaction to seeing her list of credits. Yet the woman had been great! No doubt about that. He'd have to toss her name to Gene.

No, maybe not just that, but a little bit more.

He'd see she got something for her efforts. Obviously Gloria could act up a storm—well, good enough to pass a normal screen test. And with her body offered-up in the right way it would hardly hurt the film. Plus the screen test would be a good ad to all the other guys who wanted a fancy new joy to enjoy.

He made a mental note to let Gene in on her bag of couch tricks. He deserved the return favor! The man had literally handed Connie over to him in such a classy way. But that was Bass. A good friend and a nice guy who played the game fair all the way around. Not everybody was that clean. And Bass had been in the business a bit longer than most of those in the studio.

He felt almost guilty thinking of Gloria, or any woman for that matter, in such a cold-blooded way.

But this was the dirty underside of the business. A lot

156

of women were more than willing to trade sex for a contract or just a new connection that might be useful in the future. And the men laughingly picked up the goodies tossed their way, in return for empty promises.

Alice Palmer had used her body to make the right connections. And, of course, some like Judy Grant happened to be at the right place at the right time when something happened that created a black hole into which they could quickly be inserted as a quick fix. How nice for her. The timing had been perfect.

So where was that lush, lovingly delightful ball of joy now? Certainly not in his office passionately offering her endless gratitude for his help. Not that he wanted her around at the moment.

Still, he felt as if she'd used him and now was on to better things. Smart kid!

That, somehow made him feel somewhat cheap.

Certainly the game was fairly new to him. Peter Denton had worked hard to get to this position, and he'd been a player, sure, yet not hard-balled, not cold-heartedly. Not like he was now turning into.

But Palmer's death had created a brittle reality around the world. The show must go on. People didn't really count. Just fast bucks. The movie must be finished. Don't look back, just rush forward. And take what you can get— they were all people users.

So what?

Now Judy really didn't matter all that much.

She was history.

Just like Alice Palmer!

On to the next project, next problem, next solution. And whatever women fell on to his casting couch. Why not? He hadn't made the rules. And he was a damned fool not to make the use of all the wonderful lovely toys falling his way. That was part of the perks.

Goodbye Judy. Have fun Judy. You have a new world ahead of you—you're on your way to fame!

Lovely, delicious, seductive Judy.

And I don't give a damn!

And that was rather strange. Until yesterday, he had

been fairly blowing his cork to get at her again—until he met Connie.

What the hell made her so damned special he had no way of knowing.

Yet, he had to admit, there was something about Connie and he wasn't quite able to figure it out. Nothing had been said, really. Just a quick exchange at the end. And her stunning offer to call him. How delightful. Usually it went the other way: "Don't call me, I'll call you!" But he didn't care about rules. Not when looking into her lovely eyes. As he had been doing far more than he should have, over a couple of martinis. He hadn't even touched her; yet wanted to. He wanted to get her into his arms and fairly feast on her body, devour it. He wanted to spend time with the woman, get to know her, learn about her life, what made her kick, happy, to fill her dreams with reality. To shower her with gifts.

God, you're an ass! He laughed at himself. She's just another couch trinket! Take her, use her and go on to the next toy joy that offers itself up.

Yet her imagine kept haunting him, sitting there so close, within reach, and only their eyes communicating past the verbal bull-shit they were exchanging as conversation. A contract offer, a simple spoken bribe to keep her quite long enough to get past the immediate tragic events of the day. She had been exposed to a lot of inside information that neither Bass nor him had been very smart about keeping shut-mouthed about. Yet, there was something about Connie which invited trust. It was as if they all had known one another for years and she would never reveal what had been said to anybody. Insane as that might seem, he simply knew that to be the truth. A lot of things could be communicated, silently. And that's what the woman's manner and eyes had tacitly said.

Regardless of the implications, the obvious shift in her attention from Bass to him had been starkly blunt, even if skillfully handled. The PR man's silent withdrawal had said it all. She was being delivered onto her next stepping stone to success: The Denton Couch.

That seemed cold, harsh and reality.

Yet Denton couldn't get it out of his mind. A nagging something which kept bringing her mental image flashing into being, tauntingly engaging, intelligent, even if somewhat sad—probably a natural reaction to seeing the death of Alice Palmer.

But the searing connection that had fired between them had been a soul embracing experience. Totally unsettling. She had continually floated in the background of his thoughts, last night, even while dealing with the very serious business at hand.

Now, sitting in his office, this morning, he simply submitted to a delicious mental reverie about Connie. It was a quiet moment before all hell would break loose. Nobody had arrived at the studio, yet. This was an hour to let his mind drift. And Connie Remington was his delicious escape.

He wasn't thinking of her in sexual terms so much as imagining them walking hand in hand on the beach, barefoot, the sand still warm, even though night had slipped down around the world to cast her lovely features in dim moonlight. It was a romantic setting, not a blatantly erotic scene. They weren't speaking, but his mind was frantically attempting to find the words to discover something about her life, about all of her, what she had been like as a child, what caused her to want to be an actress, how she had gotten to this place where they had met and were, now, having a chance to actually get to know one another.

Now that was insanity.

Yet it was a rather inviting setting for the obvious destination of a shared evening exploring one another through endless hours of intimacy.

A total fiction. Chances are he'd call her, set up a date and they'd end up spending the night together—at most!

He had almost forgotten her suggestion that she call him. That memory surfaced, suddenly, and made him smile.

And her last "Should I call you tomorrow?" had been stunning! Deliciously, seductively, thrilling!

Later, a short exchange with Gene about that had caused them both to chuckle.

"Is she always that bold?" he had asked the PR man.

"No. Not at all. Just a very nice lady. I was as

stunned as you were. I think she was too."

"A brazen lady, if you ask me!" Denton mused. "Really something special. Is she really all that...you don't mind...I feel like I'm stepping into your territory."

"Not at all. She's a free agent. We're good friends. You have to be realistic about such matters, Pete. That's how it is. I'm used to it."

"I suppose so," Denton nodded.

"She's a nice person, Pete."

"Aren't they all?" was Denton's flip response.

"Some are different."

They said nothing more about her after that, involved in other matters which surged around them concerning the picture and the public handling of Palmer's death.

That was last night. This was the morning and Peter Denton's musings about Connie was a mixed bag, swinging from cold user to totally school-boy crush.

He had to tell Betty to put her call right through.

Then the studio became alive. Slowly. A breakfast was ordered up and delivered, coffee, eggs and the trimmings. Betty was a perfect secretary and had sized things up the minute she arrived half an hour early from her required time. Her head had popped in through the half opened door, eyes took him in, nodded and disappeared to order the morning feed.

Then the fun began.

The phone kept him busy for a while. Then it was silent. Paper work drew his attention. Then the phone rang.

At the same time a knock came on the door, Betty was allowing somebody to enter without her escorting them. It opened to have Judy Grant step into the office.

She was smiling happily. Radiant. He had never seen her look so lovely. The bright eager look in her eyes was all loving warmth.

"Hi!" she greeted, immediately in front of the desk. "I'm reporting for duty, sir! Been meaning to thank you for what you did for me. I owe you a lot, Pete. And I've been difficult, I know. But thanks."

"Just a sec," he said to her, then into the receiver in his hand, said: "Hello?"

160

"Hello to you, too," a voice answered him. It was Connie.

CHAPTER→❷❷

When he heard Connie's voice he couldn't help feeling a pleasant thrill of surprise.

Rather nervously she quickly said: "How are you?"

"Fine, and you?"

A sudden silence met that.

"Fine."

It was all rather silly and awkward, because both of them knew the real reason for her call. He was totally surprised by his own tongue-tied response to her voice. There was a prolonged silence as he kept his eyes away from Judy's, afraid she would read his mind. The silence continued for what seemed forever, but couldn't have been more than a moment, for he heard Connie's voice say: "Look to be honest, I shouldn't have called. I know you are busy and all that. And I'm—well...never mind."

"What's that?" he managed to say, feeling his voice had dropped into a raspy whisper. The question hardly made sense, nor did the sudden confusion in his mind. He literally wanted to ask her out on a date, of all things!

And that was his problem with women—he was too soft and romantic when it came to the weaker sex. Or was it just this Connie? That didn't make sense at all. She was just one of the endless list of woman on the make to get their names famous—and men like him took full advantage of their weak positioning power. Somehow he felt cheap thinking of Connie in that light. Yet there wasn't anything in the world to suggest otherwise.

"I'm sorry, Mr. Denton..."

"Denton? Call me Peter or Pete or anything, but not Mister anything."

"We hardly know one another," she almost whispered. "I'm being silly. Okay. Peter. I called just to—"

"Glad you did!" All at once his voice gained control of his mind, and words just flowed without thought: "Look—why don't we have dinner together?"

"Tonight?" she said excitedly. No doubt she hadn't planned on his making it so easy for her—or moving so fast. Now he was on the right track. It would be interesting finding out just what this Connie had to offer. Hot licks for hot chicks on the couch.

And it wouldn't be difficult to cut some hours of free time from the Studio. Actually, things were in a stall, anyway. What needed to be done was being handled right off, smoothly, directly. Judy's presence in his office announced how smoothly the machinery was functioning.

Yes, he could set aside this evening all the time he needed to be with Connie.

He quickly said: "Why not?"

"Seven?"

"Works for me. But make it eight."

"Want my address?"

"Give it to Betty!" *And maybe into my arms.* Again he felt somehow nastily cheap at considering Connie in such a manner. But, after all, it was her game and she seemed to know the rules. Hardly a fool. Smart. Maybe even talented.

He hung up and looked up at Judy Grant. He had almost forgotten that she was standing there in front of his desk, looking and listening to his conversation.

Smiling, he stood and stepped around to her side. "Well, Judy, it looks like you got your chance."

He reached for her, but she stepped gently away.

"Not now, Peter...you'll ruin my makeup."

That was the death-sign. Denton recognized the coldness in her attitude and voice. The affair was finished. Of course. He didn't really care. It seemed as if too much had happened since they had seen each other last. Sometimes events made it impossible for people to make a go of it— even if they might be very well suited to one another.

But it was strange her abrupt change. Almost like she was saying: *"Don't need ya no mo, daddy, been fun but...well that game's over!"* It was too soon. A strange puzzle that; but not worth the effort of weeding it out.

Also, he had other things that were more important on his mind.

The first, of course, was getting Judy through the morning routine. She had to meet Van Horn. And the rest of those who would be handling her from then on.

But, regardless of all else, she was his talent discovery, and that meant more than anything to him, it would boost his career. It would place him in a powerful position in the studio. For the time being, at least, nothing could harm or be a threat to his job. He was safe.

That afternoon with Van Horn, Judy Grant was quickly pushed from one spot to another. The main thing was to keep her so busy that she didn't have time to think. Keep her hopping—then they could have her signed to a contract before she had a chance to look at the small print.

It was a dirty trick, in one way—but then they were giving her a big chance to get headed in the right direction, fast. Normally it might have taken her several years to get a part like she was being given.

Of course her agent would have the last word.

So in the long run she was way ahead.

And it was obvious that Van Horn was delighted with his "new discovery" again and again saying things like: "Now see what I've found?" and "We'll become great friends, I just know it!" He took her arm, at times, even held her hand in his. And Judy was more than attentive, making it a point to let the man know she was happy to be his center of attention. She flirted brazenly with him and every time their eyes met, it was obvious that his inner horn was blowing full blast. The man had been famous over the years in enjoying the casting couch game—and it didn't take any imagination to know where Judy Grant was headed, even before being signed to a contract.

That evening Denton would be with Connie. Their first date together. Their first really important meeting.

* * * * * * *

It was eight and Connie waited nervously for the door

bell to ring. She felt the same way she had the first evening that Gene Bass had called for her. It had been exactly the same time of night.

But tonight something special was in the offing. Nothing had really been said, but they both knew what was planned. A lot had mentally taken place between them, all but getting into bed together.

She could hardly believe how a man and woman would be total strangers one moment and then the very next feel they had known each other all their lives. Of course that didn't make any sense. But it was a gut feeling.

What about *him?*

And then there was Judy Grant. She only guessed that the woman had been seeing Denton for one purpose: and now that purpose was fulfilled.

Judy had been around so long that the only thing in her mind was finding a way—any way possible—to get to stardom. Using people, friends and making enemies—she didn't seem to care.

Her mind was swimming down a list of women.

Gloria the whoria. That blonde tramp. That was something Connie didn't want to become. Someone who just sold her body—and really for nothing, because she had nothing to offer outside of the casting couch. At least that's how she saw Gloria.

And Miss Alice Palmer. That wasn't really anything to aim for either. An actress, star or not, who had played the casting couch game to success. Yet was that what Connie wanted?

Doubts mixed with excitement. And none of it made much sense.

Peter Denton—he was the solution, she kept telling herself as if it were a mantra. A solution that made her feel still a little uneasy because she was beginning to wonder exactly *how* she felt about him.

She thought too much. She made the mistake of not just enjoying life and to hell with the end results. What would happen if she were killed right at that moment? Suddenly. Like Alice Palmer had been smashed out of existence! What kind of life had Miss Connie Remington lived?

She didn't want to turn into another Judy Grant. Bitter and hard—scheming. Even a little neurotic.

She looked at herself in the mirror, and after powdering her nose for the fifth and last time, she once more looked nervously toward the clock.

The bell rang just as she was looking back toward the mirror.

CHAPTER→❷❸

Denton had worked late at the office and it was past seven before he got home. By eight-fifteen he arrived at Connie's apartment. This, he felt certain, was going to be special. It was funny how neither had said anything about it, yet there was little doubt that he would make love to Connie this evening. And that was strange, too. He had always thought of sex as nothing more than seduction. With Connie it was different. Stupidly different. Foolish even thinking that. She was nothing but another woman falling onto the couch in desperate willingness to please a man with the power to offer her a part—maybe!

The drive to her apartment seemed to take forever. All he could think about was his building need for her. Never had he needed a woman so badly. And after a moment's thought he realized one reason the physical anxiety was so strong: The last woman he had made been with was Gloria the Stag Film Queen.

And amazing as the woman might be, the bitter taste of such empty sex without any real feelings underscoring the intimacies, had left him hungry for something far more meaningful. Not even a Judy Grant would have helped much. In fact, that woman was, actually, just a step above Gloria, only, perhaps, because she hadn't gone porno. And all the other quick tricks hankering to leap onto the casting couch simply seemed a pitiful reminder of how empty life could be without somebody to share it with, to care about.

It was funny how he had put Gloria out of his mind. He had forgotten to have Betty set up a screen test for her. He could never tell what she might be able to do on the screen, outside of screwing men for money. Chances were she was quite good, considering her past experience. And now with his first discovery, Judy Grant, he had the complete run of the studio. Van Horn would welcome any test investment he set into action.

And then there was Connie.

What about her? He knew that she wanted to get some movie work, and there wasn't any reason why he shouldn't set up a test for her, too. He had, actually, kinda promised her something along those lines. A small walk on, at least, in order to assure silence concerning all she'd heard yesterday.

He laughed as he stepped up to her apartment door. Once he'd gotten started, he was blowing crazy jazz in all directions, But one thought of caution wedged its way into his mind: *he could overdo a good thing—and that would be just too bad for Peter Denton.*

After knocking on Connie's door, he waited nervously. He was anxious see her reaction to having a screen test. He was even more eager to take her in his arms and make love to her.

Assuming that would happen. And if she gave him even a hint of warmth he'd sweep her off her lovely feet. He'd love her to death. Ravish that nice, classy bod. Carry her down the beach into the distant jungle and rediscover the virgin joy of young love.

That image jolted him. No beach, no jungle. Just the Hollywood cement canyons and fake front illusions of reality.

And in this land, love was the last thing anybody had in mind. They were all raging beauties tossing their real or surgically enhanced charms in rapid sensation into arms of user males with hands out to collect all their goodies for a fast spin.

A strange idea crossed his mind.

Any woman was good in a pinch—but when you were in love it was a different matter!

That made all the difference in the world.

The thought shook him up a little bit. He hardly knew Connie, and he had no reason to think that he held any affection toward her.

After all, she had been handed over by Gene Bass,

like a class-A prime piece of meat.

This fact made him go cold inside. Connie having been Bass' toy. And handed over like a gift on a platter. Just because he was an assistant producer? No! That wasn't any reason at all. At least he hoped not. And Eugene Bass for all his quiet manner, and decency, was a player, too.

One thing that he knew about Connie: she had been the one to make the first move.

The door opened and for a long moment he just stood there, looking at her. She was so beautiful. Breathtaking in a manner he hardly expected. It felt as if somebody had smashed his gut, paralyzed his lungs. Class, sex and intelligence all packaged into one lovely young lady.

"Hello," Connie purred, letting the corners of her lips turn up into a pleasant smile. "Come on in."

For a second he couldn't move. Just looking at her was pure heaven.

Her dress squeezed and flared. Her body seemed almost nude before his eyes. The top of the silky cloth hardly hid her breasts which were full and supple looking, but over-ripe and voluptuous like Gloria's. They were round and brimming.

Then her waistline was narrow and pinched in so that the flaring shape of her hips circled artistically down toward shapely legs.

He could hardly wait to get that sensual and beautiful form in his arms.

Denton stepped forward and closed the door behind him. Then he reached for her. But she glided away.

"My, aren't you the eager beaver!" she laughed throatily.

"Well, can you blame me?"

"Not my fault! I'm just an innocent young lady. And I simply don't know what I'm doing. Is that okay with you?" The teasing gleam in her eyes was more than an open invitation to continue the matter, but he let it lay there where she had dropped it. There was plenty of time for loving—later in the evening.

And strangely enough it wasn't important at that moment. Enough for her to know how stunning he thought she was.

"Can I offer you anything?" she asked, picking up her purse.

"A leading question, that!" Mentally he added: *Everything you have! Please if there's a God in the sky.*

"I think we best be on our way." She nodded to the front door. "Out, James."

* * * * * * *

The next hours were a whirl to Connie. She continued to feel light headed while near him. The drinks, of course, helped to offer up a relaxing mood, a sense of comfort. In fact she felt very comfortable with this man she hardly knew, yet felt as if she'd known him all her life.

Could that be some kind of love? She wondered throughout dinner, finding it hard to keep her eyes off him as they talked and ate.

"I hope you like the steak," he had asked, "I didn't considered ..."

"No, you recommended and I accepted," was all she said. Actually he had almost ordered the complete meal without consulting her: Double Cut Filet Mignon, Sauce Béarnaise, baked potatoes and mixed green vegetables, all preceded by a lovely shrimp cocktail, with Rose Wine and a lovely salad, lightly touched with a special house dressing. All of it was served elegantly by their waiter and his assistant. The lights were low and soft.

"They have a pretty nice combo for dancing," he noted, "I take it you like to dance?"

"Why, of course." In fact she would have faked it in order to be taken into his arms on the dance floor. "I've always loved dancing. All kinds. Even swing!"

"Great! Not only the combo is great, but the feature singer is super! She appears with a number of big swing dance bands."

"You know her?"

"Not really. But we've crossed paths. She has done some film work. So ...But it is her voice that's really great. Not only does she look super on the stage, she's a lovely lady off-stage, too."

"You're into the music scene, then?" she inquired, surprised. "I mean, you really like it."

"Sure. Especially jazz and Big Bands. I was born too late. Back in the forties or fifties the big bands were really Big. Glenn Miller, of course. Stan Kenton. Benny Goodman. Artie Shaw. Les Brown. Ray Anthony … Wish I could have seen them. Only thing left are the recording, the list goes on. But no time now for that or other things." He shrugged. "Show-biz business is…time consuming."

"But, I notice, you have time for…" she smiled, "dating."

"Another issue."

"I bet you meet a lot of lovely ladies just clamoring for your attention." That was an impulsive statement she wished she hadn't made. She was always impulsive at the wrong time; and especially after a couple of drinks.

"Well, not as lovely as you, Connie."

She felt a blush race up her cheeks and looked away, embarrassed. "I…well…thank you, I guess.'"

"Just guess?"

And the conversation continued on to other subjects, which revealed they both had a lot of mutual interest, in tennis, movies, music, even the arts. Connie said: "I haven't seen any real art shows since coming to California."

"Well, maybe I could take you to some."

They both loved the ocean. And the mountains. Skiing.

At one point he insisted that she reveal her who life to him. "I want to know all about you. Everything. What you like. What you hate. What you want in life. What you…"

"Just that? So little?" she actually laughed.

"Well, tell me something about your childhood, and…well, how you got here, and why…oh, forget it. Just tell me all about you."

But that never happened because he noted the time and told her it was getting close to nine.

"You turn into a pumpkin at nine—I thought that happened to Cindy at twelve midnight!"

"Hardly. But the band plays on. They'll start in a few

minutes. Then the show."

"I'd best powder my face, then."

"Or what ever you ladies do."

"What ever," she smiled, warmly. She almost danced on her to the ladies room. The only person there was a rather lovely blonde who was making a last minute check of herself in the mirror.

"I don't know," the woman said to herself, subtly adjusting the sleek black dress that hugged her lush body, "I hope that hides all the flaws."

"Flaws?" Connie couldn't help saying. The woman was stunning, and Connie instantly recognized her. "Oh, high, Nancy. We met some time ago."

"Did we?" the woman offered, still somewhat concerned with her striking image in the mirror.

"You don't remember, of course," Connie offered, and then before Nancy could say anything, continued: "You kinda gave me some advice."

Nancy looked at her, this time focusing. "I did?"

"Well, in a round about way, that is," Connie quickly said, embarrassed.

"What about?"

Now she was in for it, and said: "Well you worked for Disney, didn't you?"

"Oh, sure. When I was very young and darn lucky, too."

"That's what you said."

"A safe, wonderful place to work. Kept this girl healthy, not too wealthy, but wise to the ways of those wolves that were kept at bay."

"Yes, you said: he kept you safe from the…well, casting couch, I guess."

"I kinda remember you, now. You're an actress."

"Well, struggling. Trying my best."

"Well, keep the wolves at bay." She looked at her carefully, smiling: "You are really pretty."

"Thanks," Connie said, almost embarrassed. The woman was so open and easy to talk to.

"Just don't give up your power. Otherwise they'll just eat you as toast for breakfast and then spit you out when they're finished."

"I just wish there were more Disney-types around to protect us struggling actors."

"They're around, believe me. Just sometimes illusive."

"One feels so frustrated." She was half speaking to herself, and at the same time surprised to be so open with Nancy. A total stranger. "And powerless. I just hate being … in that trap."

"The lure can be tempting. I've told many actresses I've worked with that same thing. Just be strong."

"It can be hard…you were lucky."

"I'm not the only one. Just don't let them devour you, if you can help it."

"I won't."

"Well, gotta run. See ya around, maybe. Good luck with your career." Then the woman was gone in a flash.

Connie considered that warning. "God, I sure as hell wish I had a Disney to protect me!"

She smiled at herself. "Well, maybe Peter Denton will have to fill in, as the best I can get."

For a moment she almost laughed at herself. They were on their first date, and who knew what would follow, later. And he'd probably dump her after that.

"Oh, God, why does it have to be this way?" she wondered. Wasn't there some way to avoid that horrid Hollywood game.

Well, Nancy, whoever she was, had managed.

The advice to be strong was right on!

But how can I in his *arms,* she wondered.

If they had met socially, without any professional connections, if he was just a man who had been introduced to her in some respectable, conventional way, she'd have helplessly swooned into his arms. She'd been overwhelmed when he had looked into her eyes at Gene Bass' beach house. She'd felt the thrill of that connection reach her inner core so powerfully that it was dazzling.

"Oh, come on, Connie. Grow up!"

But the very thought of being held close to Peter Denton made her feel weak all over. Just like a foolish little teenager.

Well, girl, you ain't no bloody teenager. Be strong!

Connie turned away from the mirror and then went back to the table, where Peter was waiting.

The combo was already playing dance music and he stood and literally glided her towards the dance floor without a word.

The minute their bodies came in contact all the inner rationalizations to be strong were melted away. In an instant Connie knew it would be impossible to resist this man. She could hardly keep from clutching to him; but she did manage to remain politely formal in those first moments.

The music was light and enjoyable. Half dance, half jazzy and when the swing tempo came, she discovered that he was a divine dancer, and they flowed together as if being lifted on some ocean wave. The music itself was driving them along the dance floor. One dance flowed into the next.

Then suddenly the music stopped.

The drummer, who headed the combo, was speaking and said: "And now, ladies and gentlemen, The Club Electra has the joy of presenting a really class act! We're now delighted to presents the lovely *Swinging Nancy Osborne!*"

Connie watched as a lovely blonde woman moved quickly on stage.

"Thank you, Johnny," she said to the drummer, then turned to audience. "What a great place this is!"

This was the Nancy she'd been talking to early in the lady's room.

After a few more opening comments, Nancy turned towards the combo, hand just slightly moving to offer the beat, then as the music started, and after a quick few bars she sang: "*Five...six...seven...eight!*"

The opening number was "All That Jazz" and it really swung up a storm.

Then Nancy went into a very slow rendition of "Tenderly."

Connie felt the man pull her very close for the first time. She simply wanted to throw her arms around his neck, drape herself all over him. Somehow she managed to simply follow his lead. They started swaying to the music, just

174

standing there in each others arms, and she simply let herself melt against him. Then at the end of the song, she felt his lips gently press her cheek with a soft kiss. It was all she could do to control the urge to find his lips with hers. It continued like that even in the more up tempo songs, neither of them wanting to part. Then Nancy sang a lovely romantic ballad, *I Know Why* and Peter whispered in her ear: "Oh, I love this song. Years ago Glenn Miller introduced it. Not many people know it." They clung close together, cheek to cheek throughout the song. At the end he pulled back, and suddenly their lips met. It was a soft, warm, deliciously tender kiss, but fired the very core of her being. They continued dancing until the set ended and they returned to the table.

Surprisingly enough, Nancy came over to their table on her way out of the room. The singer nodded to Connie, smiling.

"You were great!" Connie offered, uncertain what to say.

"Well, thank you," Nancy replied, as she glanced at Peter, as if sizing him up. "Now don't you forget what I said…"

Her eyes finished the statement without verbalizing it.

Be strong.

Then she was gone.

"What was that all about?" Peter asked. "I didn't know you knew each other."

"We don't, really. She was in the Lady's room. We talked a bit."

"Oh? I'm impressed!"

"I didn't have any idea who she was." Luckily the subject was dropped and she didn't have to find some way of avoiding his question about her conversation with the singer.

Connie tried to tell herself to be strong, but knew that was quite impossible. She could hardly wait to leave the place. Peter paid the bill and then took her hand in his, giving it a gentle squeeze which sent a thrill through her so intense that she merely floated along side him to the car.

* * * * * * *

For Peter the evening was just one stunning moment after another. He couldn't get enough of Connie. She was breathtaking in his arms. By the time they arrived at her apartment, it wasn't even necessary to ask. She gave him her key, he opened the door and escorted her in, as if it were his own pad. They both knew what must follow, for the dance which and started earlier now demanded a total completion.

The minute the door closed he pulled her close to him. It was their first real full blown kiss, and all hell broke.

Her lips trembled open under his and he felt the excited throb of her tongue as it moved rapidly against his own. Her body pressed against him and he felt the beating of her heart under the full surge of her breast.

She pulled away and moved to the kitchen, stumbling in the dark.

A few moments later she returned with a bottle of wine and two glasses. Plopping down on the sofa in the middle of the room, she called over to him. "Why don't you join me?"

She handed him a half-filled glass of wine, and they saluted.

"To us," he offered.

"Yes. I like that," she murmured, eyes reaching up and literally caressing deeply into his very soul, it seemed.

"To us," he repeated, as he sat down very close to Connie. He held her hand in his, wanting to simply caress it tenderly, kiss it, press the fingers against his cheek. So many things he wanted to do, but instead just sat there next to her in the wonderment of what they were sharing, experiencing.

Then he put his arm around her shoulder, and she hugged gently to him, again murmuring so softly, so contently. Neither of them spoke, but merely became used to the sensation of such quite intimacy. The way she leaned against him it was impossible to keep from running his hand along the full supple swell of her breast.

A sigh moved past her lips as he pulled the strap of her dress down.

She smiled up at him, so beautiful, so loving, so invitingly. The top of her dress fell away, exposing her breasts

176

which stood there so lovely that it took his breath away for a moment.

"You're so beautiful," he managed in a choked voice.

"I won't break!" she whispered. "I promise…"

Connie almost purred in pleasure as her arms slipped around his neck. It was a soft sigh of total contentment that surged through her whole body as she clung to him.

Now he was literally overwhelmed by how wonderful she really felt next to him. Holding her close he could smell the delicate scent of perfume, as his lips caressed her creamy white throat.

A soft murmur of pleasure sounded from Connie and she squeezed closer.

He stood and lifted her into his arms. She nodded with her head, indicating a closed door, then just nuzzled her face against his, brushing her lips along his cheek as he carried her into the bedroom.

A moment later the world clouded around them, and only the awareness of one another seemed real.

CHAPTER→❷❹

To Connie that first evening with Denton seemed more like a dream than reality. Everything happened—and neither seemed to be aware of the fact that nothing had really been said about their plans or any arrangements settled. They had both expected to make love—words weren't necessary. When the moment came suddenly into being they didn't realize how quickly it had taken place. It seemed right. And that was all that really counted. Adults were like that. They didn't have to plan ahead whether there would be a goodnight kiss at the lady's door—or a good morning embrace in her bedroom the next day. It didn't matter—what happened would happen regardless.

So it had.

Simple, direct and quickly. Then later more slowly.

Connie had never felt toward any other man the way she did toward Denton. And that was one thing she couldn't understand. She had always been proud of her sexual control, but with Denton there was no control, no will for control, and no desire for control. She wanted to be made love to over and over, until exhaustion took her muscles and nerves and enfolded them into a blanket of restful, black sleep. And in his arms she was continually floating on in electric pleasure. She had experienced prolonged orgasms before, but nothing like this lingering endless wave building and building time and again, surging around her so powerfully at times that she wanted to sob and cry and knew she must be doing just that and not caring how it sounded to him, not caring if the whole world might hear. She simply wanted to wrap herself around him in every possible way and never let go.

178

It was in the morning, after Denton had left for the studio, that Connie began to think. She began to look at herself much more honestly than she ever had before in her life.

Maybe it was because of what had taken place in Denton's arms. She had experienced more than mere passion, a lustful using of her body. There had been an overwhelming sense of the man giving, not wanting to take, merely to continually give her more and more of his love. And for some insane reason it felt just like that. The total offering of a man without an ego involve, none of the showmanship grand play attempting to announce to the woman what a great big wonderful stud he was. No, with Peter Denton she had felt as if being held in the arms of a personal protector, a man who cared so deeply that he would sacrifice everything just to give without strings to the woman he loved.

And that simply made no sense at all.

Yet, rational or not, she had felt warmth, comfort—security. The emotional need to become a big name star had lost all its meaning. The only thing that seemed to count then was the need to make Peter Denton happy.

And that was down right madness.

Oh, the joy of such madness, of having somebody who could be the center of her life, somebody who would want to share all they were and could ever be in the future with her. The idea of a fantasy romance with a perfectly wonderful guy. Whom she knew totally nothing about!

They were utter strangers who had balled each other's brains out on their first date.

What must he think of her, now. Just another addition to his casting couch counter. Just another number to feed his over-bloated male ego.

Just another of a long list of easy women standing eagerly in line for their momentary chance at just a small connection with somebody important enough to pull the right strings. And the only strings were those which stripped them bare naked.

That was a blow not only to her pride and personal ego but to her very reason for living. She had thought that show business and a movie career was the most important thing in the world. She had believed that she could never be happy doing anything else. But now there was that other emotion.

Maybe it had been the drinks? The physical need for a man—Denton.

On the other hand, it could be something more meaningful, something that went deeper and was lasting.

Lasting until he walked out of the apartment.

"You're a stupid little innocent quickly becoming a toy for the Hollywood young studs. If you don't watch out you'll end up as one of those Sunset Strip hookers."

She didn't like that thought and with all her willpower she forced it to disappear down underneath the endless series of other ideas and concepts and dreams and fears.

What about Bass? She suddenly realized how safe and secure she'd felt with him. Sure he'd handed her right over to Peter Denton. But he'd also said to call him any time.

Maybe she would. They could talk rather honestly about a lot of things. He was a good friend.

Slowly Connie sank into a chair, looking blankly across tile room. She didn't see the walls or any of the furniture. All she saw were the faces of two men:

Bass and Denton—and she wondered about herself.

Was she only using Denton like she had used Bass?

In any case, that might be delusional. Chances were just the opposite with them being the pros in this nasty little game.

She hoped not. She didn't like to think she could fool herself. She didn't like that idea at all.

What she wanted to believe was that Eugene Bass was a really true friend and that Peter Denton a truly wonderful man, a divine lover and somebody who could really have an important place in her future. And not just her career.

How we can fool ourselves, Connie thought, only half-way annoyed. *But what a beautiful dream!*

CHAPTER→❷❺

For Peter Denton the next days became a mad house. The evening with Connie was his last moment of peace. His date with her had been wonderful. He was feeling happier than he'd felt for months. Connie was like a never-ending powerful cocktail—she made a man drunk with happiness and desire. And she did more than that to him. She was something suddenly important; more important than anything else. Than his job. His Great Judy Grant Discovery. Anything! And he didn't know why, and most of all he didn't care trying to think about it.

The evening before had made it final and complete. The feel of her body as it surged against his. Her lips, moist and silky, giving and eager. Her soft velvet flesh and full, supple breasts. Never had he really known a woman quite like Connie. She had such a beautiful form and figure that it made his throat choke with emotion. And the way she used it against his as the two of them had frantically and desperately sought closer union. She was everything he ever wanted in a woman!

Love at first sight. Hardly. Yet much the same thing. Love at first really true connection and communication. Love at first intimacy. Love that could be but a flash or might be something far more, far longer lasting. A meaningful relationship, no matter what. And that really yanked the ceiling away and the floor out from under him every time he let himself even think about her.

What was she doing right then?
What did she like for breakfast?
What were her favorite things to do?
Where did she like to go on vacations?

181

What had her childhood been like?

What about her parents?

What, what and then want again. It all kept teasing him with longing to know more, discover everything possible until this sudden interest was fully satisfied. If it ever could be.

Was that love?

If not, it was certainly fascination and obsession to a startling level.

And he planned on playing that game out to its final card, moment, for whatever it took.

The next couple of weeks moved quickly for Denton. It seemed that once Alice Palmer was dead most of the studio problems had smoothed out—for a while, anyway. Judy Grant and Victor Bolton worked well together and Van Horn couldn't have been more pleased. In fact the man was delighted.

But there were other problems. Personal.

He had expected that once Judy Grant got a contract she'd have been passionately throwing herself into his arms, bubbling with joyful gratitude. But nana! Before Connie that would have been quite frustrating. But the woman had simply disappeared out of his life. The only thing bothersome there was the sense of being rejected. Normally it went the other way. Now he knew the pain a lot of women were experiencing from the men who used them.

The picture was moving along so well that he was able to leave the director in complete charge. Nothing more had happened to cause a delay, and the shooting schedule was actually running ahead of time. Van Horn was more than delighted about the acting ability of Denton's *new* "discovery."

"She's great!" Myron told him one afternoon. "Two or three takes at most and we have a scene—even the most difficult. Most are done in one take. Where the hell have you been keeping her?"

Van Horn was even more excited. "Denton, my boy, you've done a great service to the studio. If there's anything you want me to do, Sweetheart, just name it. We have a great star here in Judy Grant. And the way our lawyers have her signed, sealed and legally delivered, we'll make a fortune with her."

Of course her acting ability was secondary to the way she looked on the screen.

Never had things been running better. And maybe that was the trouble. He had plenty of time to think things over—to wonder *why* there wasn't any more trouble. He had a chance to see for the first time a few things that hadn't been too obvious before.

The threatening "crank" notes. *Who had sent them: and why? Nothing seemed to fit.*

And Alice Palmer's death. Had that really been an accident?

The official police statement had read, that it was. But why the threatening notes—and then the accident? It seemed too strange to be coincidence. Yet that might have happened. Crank notes—then an accident,

The thing that was surprising though was that none of this really mattered.

And that was all because of Connie.

She was much more important. It was strange how things were working out for the two of them.

"Get Myron on the line," Denton told his secretary. "No, make that Lloyd."

A moment later he was talking to the first camera-man. "Look Lloyd, I have a favor to ask you. I know you're working with Judy Grant, but this will take only a little time. I figured only take two or three hours. This Saturday. Can you be free then?" He explained he wanted the man to do a test for an actress.

"Anything serious?" was the question offered up.

"Well, I think so." Denton offered, not certain, exactly, how the man had meant that.

"Sure. Anything to do you a favor." The man chuckled. "Ol' vanny boy is simply delighted you're your discover—and if you have more of the same thing…well, you'll own the studio!"

"Hardly. But thanks. She's a special woman. I think you'll find her…worth your top efforts!"

"Anything to please!" the man promised.

"Thanks," he said, closing the cell phone in his hand.

He looked up to see Gene Bass stepping into his office. "Where have you been keeping yourself lately."

"Around—say, I have something I wish you would arrange for me. Important!"

"Sure—shoot away."

Bass lit a cigarette and then sat in the chair opposite Denton. "It's a screen test."

For a moment Denton thought he must be kidding. Then the serious expression in Bass' eyes held back the inner laughter that was beginning to well up inside him. "Sure, why not?"

There was an awkward silence.

"Who's the girl" Denton wanted to know.

"Gloria La Sota."

It was a second or two before Denton was completely convinced that Bass was quite serious. "When did you two start up?"

"You gave me her cell phone. Remember? After you began taking Connie out. I figured that since you have too many women I might as well take a few away from you."

"I really like Connie. A lot."

"I figured. She's very special."

"But I did feel kind of guilty—"

"Stop it! Women! Who are they? Dime a million. And after all, Gloria is probably more my type."

Denton knew that wasn't the truth, but he didn't say anything about it. "Okay, more than willing to help out a few friends in need."

"This is the real thing, Pete. I think the lady has talent. From the things she's done...the latest ones. You should see them. Very artistic. Done by her own company. And lots of storyline surrounding all the sex scenes. She's really quite talented. And she has plenty of hard cash from the profits. Some women, like her, start in porno, but become big money makers, stars in their own right. Some manage to slip into legit. It is an old story. One lady, to remain unnamed, was famous for having started with stag films and then became very famous, a Super Star. She paid a lot of money to get the original negs of those stag films. Not all the prints were lost.

An old story. Never mind who. Anyway, Gloria is wanting to get legit and I think, maybe, she has a chance. Even it not, she's one hell of a doll in bed. But I assume you know all about that. I went one wild weekend with her at the beach. She knows more tricks than Carter has pills. You know, the Dr. Carter has pills to hand out…oh, never mind, no doubt long before your time. Anyway, I devoured a bit of her rather porn samples! A clip from one of her promo DVDs would be enough to sell the Horn blower. But I think we could come up with something a bit more impressive. If you know what I mean."

"Well. I guess you know what you're talking about."

"I do. And I saw her in a play. Nothing major. Just small theater, down in Santa Monica. She's not all that bad. With a little help, maybe there's hope. And with that body and her willingness to do anything on or off the screen, I do believe the Big Guy will be delighted to have her signed up for a future production."

"Okay. Okay. Tell you want. I'm setting up something for Connie. Why don't you use the same set— say an hour after we're through. It shouldn't take me more than an hour and a half—I just set up Lloyd to take care of the camera work—in fact *why* couldn't we get some scene from a script which could use both girls at once?"

For a long time the two of them thought that over. Then Bass jumped to his feet.

"Why not?" He extended his hand, "Thanks a lot!"

When Bass turned to leave, Denton quickly called him back. "Say, what about the Palmer bit?"

The press agent shrugged. "Routine. The media have the official studio report—which says nothing about the threatening notes. They already knew about the first one, but we're closed on the other two letters. No sense making a mountain out of the thing. There's no doubt that the letters were crank and that the accident was just that! The police are satisfied." His voice sounded strangely tight and nervous.

"Well, I guess it's been quite a grind—"

"More than that! A pain in the neck. I never liked Alice Palmer on the screen or off, and in the last few weeks I've had to tell the world what a wonderful person she was—

it's a lot of crap! But now the studio has other things to worry about. The talent hunt is out. All PR bull. That'll last a few weeks. Then be dropped with our discovery of the new Star at Van Horn Studios! Too many people had to be in on the Judy Grant bit, so we figure to let it all fly away. Admit it was a stunt. Nobody will care after the late news."

"I know—it was my idea. Not necessary. All that really counts is that we got a wonderful replacement for Palmer in the picture.

"And talking about our replacement. Have you seen her lately?"

Bass looked at Denton for a long time without saying anything. Then after a while he smiled. "I hear she's coming along pretty well—but...what's this about her and Van Horn and Bolton?"

For a moment Denton didn't get it.

"Where you been?"

"Well the picture is working out so well, I've left it up to Lloyd—"

"That was a mistake!"

"What the hell!"

"Haven't you heard that Judy's been running around with Van Horn now?"

Denton just stood there. For some reason he couldn't think of anything to say.

"I thought the ol' fella was past all that!"

Bass laughed. "Are you kidding. He screws them all and then dumps the leftovers our way. Well, some he doesn't even touch. But the juicy little bits he feeds into his couch like twigs...well, he probably feeds on Viagra!"

They both laughed at that, nervously, though. There was just an undercurrent of tension in Bass' eyes as he said: "And Victor Bolton and Judy are having one hell of a time at it! Too. They were an also ran. A long-time connects between them."

That figured. Now that Denton thought about it.

In fact—now that he thought about it he saw a lot of things...too many!

Just then the phone on his desk rang. "Hello?"

"Okay, Sweetheart, come on over!"

186

It was Van Horn, and from the tone of his words, Denton knew that trouble was headed his way! He felt the grinding ulcer start its imaginary activity in his stomach. Whatever was wrong must be pretty bad. Enough to make Van Horn "blow his cork!"

CHAPTER→26

The room was silent. Not a word had been spoken for several minutes. Denton was still having difficulty realizing the truth of what had taken place. He sat stone-faced, not looking at anything or anyone.

Van Horn sat at his desk, blowing smoke from the large cigar which his thin lips were clamping around. His face was set in shock, but there was an inner fury of disgust and concern shadowed in his eyes.

It was three hours after that phone call which had rushed Bass and Denton to the Big Man's private office. At that time, Van Horn was frantically waving his hands in all directions at once.

"What the hell's going on in the world!" he shouted. "I can't even make a movie without a lot of trouble. I don't get it. I don't get it at all!"

Bass and Denton just stood looking at the other man, shock working their features into stone.

"All I want to do is make a picture! And what do I get? Tell me, Sweethearts! What happens? Everything. Just everything!"

He circled around his desk and picked up a piece of paper. "Take a look at this! Just take a look at it!" He threw the paper at Denton. "Take a look at this, Sweetheart!"

"Denton caught the envelope and opened it. There was a note. It was strangely like the three that had been sent to tell everybody to stop the picture or Alice Palmer would be killed.

This one read: *Judy Grant is a dead woman if she continues making this picture!*

Denton handed the note over to Bass, who hardly

looked at it.

"What are we going to do?" he asked Van Horn.

"What are we going to do? What are we going to?" the producer screamed, each time louder. "That's what I pay you to find out, Sweetheart. *You* have to tell me. Get this off by back! I can't have another murder—who's out to get me—*who?"*

"Don't you think we should call the police in this time?" Denton suggested softly.

Bass spoke up then. "No! Hell no! That's all we need. If there's anything behind this it shouldn't be hard to track down."

Denton turned to the press agent. "You kidding?"

Bass shrugged. "Why should I kid you?"

"Come on, Sweetheart, out with it!"

"Well, for one thing—" His voice broke off. A smile showed through the tightness of his lips. "Let's say that somebody here at the studio was trying to put pressure on—"

"On what?" Denton wanted to know. He couldn't see what Bass was getting at.

"Well, don't you think that it's rather strange that somebody has been sending letters to us on this particular movie? Why this movie?"

An idea sank in. Denton felt a nervous twitching in his stomach.

"Why *this* particular movie?" he repeated. That was a good question. One that had nagged him, too. Things like this had never happened before. Oh crank letters, sure. Email was a cess-pool of such stuff. But not ones that continued— and not ones that came true. Maybe the Palmer "accident" really hadn't been one after all. Maybe it had been planned murder. But *why?*

Van Horn spoke up. "But what you're saying is that Alice Palmer was killed—murdered!"

"I'm not saying it!" Bass told him, tapping the note in his hand.

Denton offered: "No! He's not saying it. He doesn't *have* to! The note says it all. As simple as that!"

"Oh, come on, Sweethearts! What you trying to tell me?"

"That somebody wants to ruin this movie for you. Or ruin *Calvin 'Van Horn Productions"* Denton announced. "Or it meaningless."

The silence was shocking. Nobody said anything for a long time; all were trying to figure out who and what and why there could be any reason to attempt to ruin the Palmer-Grant movie.

"What about Judy? Don't you think we should tell her about the notes?" Denton asked.

Bass slowly shook his head from side to side.

"Why not? She has a right to know!"

Van Horn leaned over his desk and spoke into the small intercom.

"Send the Grant girl over here!" he ordered.

The three of them settled down in chairs and waited in silence for Judy Grant to arrive.

Denton's mind was beginning to flash through the last few weeks. Starting from that first day that Van Horn had called him over to the studio to hear about the first threatening note to Alice Palmer.

The more he thought about it all, the more unsettled he felt. Things which he hadn't noticed before started becoming very important. It was surprising how a person could be so blind during the time an event was taking place. Only later, after the dust and fog of the moment had vanished, everything fell into place.

It seemed like only a few moments before Judy arrived. She was bright and happy, smiling and bubbling. "Hi! How's everybody!"

Her eyes took in the room, narrowed. The three men were very serious, grim and she picked up on it instantly.

Then, as Van Horn stood and indicated a chair for her to sit, she became deathly serious. "What's wrong? What happened?"

"Now just take it easy, Sweetheart. There's nothing to be worrying about."

That was a lie if Denton had ever heard one! Not even an understatement.

For a moment nobody said anything; it was as if each were waiting for the other to start. Denton didn't want to be

190

the one to tell Judy about the note. Yet, now that he thought of it, maybe it was his job.

He stood and turned toward the young woman. "Judy."

"Yes!" she said a little too loud, eyes snapping to his.

"I think you had...well, take a look at this." He looked nervously around for the note. Bass had placed it on the desk. After a moment he handed it to Judy.

Her face frowned as she started reading to herself. Then her eyes widened in alarm. Shock drained her face of all color.

"But...but it can't be! It can't!" she yelled, looking up at Denton. "This must be some kind of trick! Yes. Just a trick. Gag. Nothing. What could it be? You aren't taking it seriously, are you? Just a horrid, perverse joke! *What the hell else could it be?*"

Her face started to look oddly crafty. "That's it. You almost had me fooled." She laughed a bit shrilly, then waved the note in front of her. "What a gag! You had for a moment."

A forced sounding giggle came from Judy. It didn't ring true. But, of course she must be experiencing some very complex reactions to this new threat. The poor girl must be terrified.

"I get it, now. Of course, one of *you* wrote it!" She didn't seem to be aware that she was talking out loud. "Yes one of you must have done it! I'm convinced of it! That's it. Of course."

That last continued to sound more like inner thoughts being verbalized.

"What do you mean?" Denton demanded, trying hard to understand what she was getting at. His hands were on her shoulders, squeezing hard.

"Don't you understand?" Judy asked, looking pitifully up at Denton; and then her expression changed, hardening.

"You stupid fools!" She pulled away from him. Then a burst of harsh laughter, bitter sounding, followed. "Men. You all think alike. You use us as toys to feed your egos to get off on, but to you we aren't human, we aren't people. All we are things. Just things. And you play dirty with your filthy little lies. And your crappy demands. And handouts as if … you all make me sick."

She glared savagely at their stunned expressions. "Surprise, surprise. *Sweethearts*! Who do you think wrote those letters? The man in the moon?"

She tossed her hands in the air, crying: "Stupid, stupid, stupid! All of you! Look at the expressions on your faces! Just a trio of bloody pricks!"

The woman's face was contorted in rage. "And I bet none of you have guessed the truth. Or maybe one of you has. I don't know. Don't care. You're crap! All of you!"

"Judy," Bass muttered, being the first one to break the silence which followed her outburst.

Van Horn recovering, fairly screamed, standing behind his desk, "How dare you speak to me like that. After you've been in *my* bed. You dare to talk that way to me? What's wrong with you? Have you gone insane?"

"Hardy, Sweetheart," she literally snarled. "And I'm not stupid, either."

Denton soothed, "What's going on, Judy. Why the outburst?"

It didn't make sense.

Her eyes literally snapped in his direction. "You shits! You don't think I wrote that note do you?"

They gaped at her. Stunned.

"Oh, God! You stupid jerks. Well, I didn't! You can believe that. I didn't write this one…"

"Who the hell," Van Horn blurted, "said you did?"

"Oh, don't give me that sweet crap." Her voice was shrill, she was screaming into the air, eyes flaring from one man to the other. "I know you're filthy little minds, *all* of you. Think you're so smart. Think you can run us around your fingers. Well, you're stupid. Down right stupid. Dumb. Dumb bloody asses!"

She waved her arms in the air, then cupped her hands under her breasts. "Give you one of these…And so easy to twist around. Wave a booby in your face and you're hard up for a…oh you all make me sick. Fuck all of you! How stupid can you get? *I wrote those other notes—*"

192

Her voice broke off. Shock whitened her face.

Hard, endless sounding silence shattered the room like a bomb had been exploded there.

Judy was standing rigidly, eyes still glued to Denton's. She wasn't even breathing, her lips were half open, and then finally they snapped shut.

Obviously she had realized what she had just admitted.

The shock value of that last sentence left everybody numb. She was, strangely enough, the first to recover, then hell broke loose.

Judy muttered something that sounded like *I'll get the bastard*!

Before they could recover, she had whipped around and run from the office.

Van Horn was the first to overcome his shock. He simply screamed so that his secretary could hear: "Get the studio Security on the phone. Hold Judy Grant—don't let her off the lot!"

Denton just sat there, not able to think about anything except what Judy had just admitted. He was trying to fit that fact together with all the rest. It didn't figure. It didn't figure at all.

And worst of all: *who wrote the last note?*

Obviously Judy hadn't. Her outburst had been not so much a confession but a horrified scream of confused realization!

That was the biggest puzzle of all!

CHAPTER ➔ 🌑 🌕

Surprisingly enough, Judy Grant got out of the studio before anybody could stop her. After that it was only a matter of calling the police and waiting for them to pick her up.

In the meantime Van Horn, Bass and Denton sat waiting in the producer's office. Nobody said anything. There just wasn't anything to be said. Conversation at this point would only confuse matters more. Judy Grant was the only person who might be able to give them an idea who had sent this last note. She was the only person who might know why it had been sent. The fact that she was involved with the first threats against Alice Palmer, stunningly dramatic as it was, hardly touched on her reaction to this last one. Up until her outburst the woman had been safely secured behind an unsolved mystery. Now she had ripped that mask away—and anything might happen.

So they waited in a silent room.

It was late when Denton drove home. The police hadn't been able to find Judy Grant and Van Horn had finally given up waiting, simply stating: "Let the authorities weed it out. We'll just have to take it on the chin. One has to know when to withdraw and pay the price. I'm tired. Go home, the two of you. Get drunk. I don't care. Just get back here bright and early. Maybe by then things will have settled a bit."

Strangely enough the producer had not pointed a finger at Denton to say he was responsible for everything, that he'd been the one to bring her to the attention of the studio, that she was his discovery. Yet that was a bottom line that would surely slam his budding career with a death blow.

Denton was emotionally exhausted when he opened

194

the door and walked into his front room. He was too tired to notice that the lights were already on. He actually didn't notice anything at first. Then a voice broke through his thoughts.

"I wondered when you'd get here!" He recognized the voice as Judy's.

That was shock number one.

The second was when he looked up and saw the beautiful nude form of the young woman stretched out on the long, low sofa. Most of all what caught his attention was a hard, cold, calculating and hateful expression in her otherwise lovely eyes.

The third jolt was what she was holding in her hand: A small black revolver. It was pointed in his direction. Her lips smiled nastily as she leaned forward slightly, positioning her body so that he had a full view of its curving perfection.

"See what you missed?" she cried. "You could have had me—all of me! If you hadn't been so smart. Everything was going fine...until you refused to help me out on my career. I couldn't wait around while you used my body toys to play your filthy little games. I wanted in, this time. I wanted my chance. So I had to take other steps. I had to see to it that Alice Palmer didn't make the movie. I wanted my big break and I knew you would see to it that I got it—if for no other reason than that you wanted *me*!"

That was insane. She must be out of her bloody mind; completely lost in some horrid fantasy hell.

The three surprises had numbed his mind for only a split second, and now he was thinking things out so fast it made him slightly dizzy. Even the threat of the gun didn't seem to mean anything to him right then. Instead he was beginning to see things quite clearly for the first time. All the events of the past few weeks flashed across his memory.

Judy Grant getting mad because he hadn't suggested that Van Horn give her a screen test. No reason just mad. Then the way she broke things off—no reason! How everything had worked out so well for her.

But it didn't figure. He didn't know why, but nothing really added up at all.

"I'm going to kill you, Mister Peter Denton!" Judy

shouted at him, half standing and starting to move in his direction. "I'm going to kill you because of what you've done to me. To all of us. What all of you did, do and will continue to do…unless I kill you! That'll end all the little games you play!"

"Look—wait a minute."

"Why? Why should I wait? After you tried to scare me with a phony crank letter just because you got jealous of how fast I was moving up? Because I was banging the ol' man?"

"You think I wrote that?" he gasped. "You're mad!"

"Right. I'm furious! You thought you could outsmart me. You stupid little man!" She stood, gun still held firmly in her right hand.

"I *didn't* have anything to do with writing that letter. Nothing at all!" Even in his desperate mental anxiety it was hard to keep his eyes off the lovely sway of Judy's naked breasts as they moved with every step she took.

"Oh go to hell!" she told him. "Go on to hell!"

"Listen, I'm telling you the truth. Somebody must know about what you did—or is taking advantage of the situation! Believe me. I didn't have anything to do with … I wanted to help you! Just believe that!"

"You wanted my body! You wanted to play lover-man with these." She looked down at her breasts, then ran a hand along her thighs. "You wanted your toy to enjoy when you snapped your fingers."

"Come on, you know better. Anyway…" He almost tossed in Connie's name to underscore his lack of interest in Judy. But the look in the woman's eyes stopped him cold. It wouldn't matter. In fact, that would simply throw acid in her face.

Judy was fairly close to him now. And the gun was pointed at his gut—unmoving.

"Come on—give a guy a chance!" he tried to reason with her. "Just believe me. We've been trying to get hold of you all afternoon."

"I was waiting right here for you. I wanted to kill you—show you how beautiful I am—make you want me like you did before you…met Connie! That little whoring tramp!

196

Slut! She's just like the rest of us. Trapped in a game you men dish out. Well, I've screwed your little couch a little differently! As to Connie…well…don't look so surprised! Of course I knew all about her. She's an old friend. I figured, good for her! She'll whore for you just like I had to. and all the others have to. She can play you like you have played so many others!"

She paused, studying him with amazement. "Oh, you sure are a sucker! Don't you know men are just big second bananas and we girls know just how to peel and devour! And it is so easy. You're just simple. Nakedly simple. Disgustingly simple. And we all know it. And the smarts ones like me…and you're darling, oh, so innocent, lovely Connie Remington knows just how to handle a jerk like you! She's twisted you right out of shape and into her hands like a stupid little boy with a school-boy crush. You all make me laugh!"

But she wasn't laughing. Instead her eyes reflected savage hatred and the gun remained solidly leveled at his gut.

He felt a sick grind explode inside. Nothing seemed quite real. She was suggesting that Connie was a lie, that she was nothing but an illusion, that what they had shared and felt was merely another kind of game, one which women knew how to play far better than men. On their playing field, men were helpless. Only on the couch did the men have ultimate power.

He didn't know what to believe any more. Other than the hard fact that Judy Grant must be quite mad and was pointing a gun at his gut and determined to make full use of it.

Desperate, he groped at a straw, forcing his voice to sound reasonable, convincing: "Come on, stop the kidding. We know you're the only one who can tell us who sent the other note. This last one!"

She looked at him strangely. The expression in her eyes revealed that she half believed what he was telling her. In that instant of indecision she lowed the gun, hand dropping to her side.

Her voice was small, thoughtful, frightened as it said:

"Then if you didn't write it...who...Vic—?"

He stood there, dazed at what had happened. The mood change in Judy's attitude was surprising. She gazed up at him, suddenly smiling warmly. "Oh, Peter, we were...so wonderful together!"

Then without warning she came close, and quite confident in her manner, slipped slender arms around his neck. "We were so wonderful together, weren't we?"

He was both stunned by this change, puzzled and totally aware of her soft, yielding flesh as it pressed up against him, urgently, almost begging.

"I did love being with you!" she murmured. "I loved you in me!"

Her body surged up against his and he found it difficult to keep from wanting to literally rape her in a savage mating. To literally ravish her flesh in an insane release of energy which had built up throughout the day and exploded into a tight knot in his gut in the last minutes. His last thought, before explosive blackness hit the back of his head was the raw, totally torrid awareness of Judy's naked body.

The black fog drifted away. It cleared with a throbbing ache which seemed to be building at the back of his skull. Then awareness popped into being.

What had happened? Where was Judy? Who had hit him?

He instantly realized the truth. She'd had the gun still in her hand when coming into his arms. That seductive body, so naked, so lush, had literally hypnotized him. Judy Grant had an overwhelming sexual energy that could turn a stone man into melted lava. No doubt about that. Pure, raw sex. And he'd momentarily submitted, instinctively reacting to the mere erotic energy she'd been able to envelop him in with that intimate embrace.

His mind suddenly became alive. The eight words flashed before his eyes.

"Then if you didn't write it who...Vic—"

Victor...*Bolton!*

The idea struck a terrifying logical chord in his mind. It would make everything tie together.

Victor Bolton!

198

He had to get to the man!

He was half way out of his apartment when he thought of the police. He grabbed his cell phone, dialed 9-1-1. "This is an emergency!" Then without thinking about it, he simply said it was a matter of life and death and gave Victor Bolton's address.

A moment later he was in his car driving as fast as the law would allow across town toward the writer's apartment.

* * * * * * *

Victor Bolton had no idea who was banging on his apartment door. It was loud and angry sounding. He was mentally locked into a scene being typed into the computer—a new script he planned on developing for the Van Horn Studios.

When he opened the door, it was somewhat of a shock to see Judy Grant standing there. She moved into the room without a word. He closed it behind her, then turned.

"What a lovely surprise," he greeted, deciding to play it cool, warm, with deep caring. Friendship and anything else necessary to play her—Judy, he knew, could be difficult—and since she'd teamed with Van Horn he hadn't seen her at all. It was quite a surprise to have her approach him. What could have gone wrong?

Then, instantly he knew, all too much, exactly what must be going on! He stared, horrified, at the woman, eyes widened in terror, as he saw the gun in her hand. A thin layer of sweat covered his forehead. "What the hell...Judy, put that damn thing down!"

Judy's lips twisted in a snarling smile. Her eyes narrowed.

"Come on, put that thing down!" Bolton cried, starting to step forward.

"Just stay where you are," Judy ordered, her lips white and thin. The gun didn't move from its direct line with his stomach.

Bolton froze. "Look—what's gotten into you!"

"You made one *big* mistake—Mister Victor Bolton,"

Judy tightly whispered in a low rasping voice. "That last letter was a very, big *bad* mistake, it cost me everything!"

Bolton looked at her for a long time and then half
smiled in contempt. "What did you expect? You were playing old man Van Horn. What kind of stupid fool do you take
me for? And anyway the note was just a joke!"

"Some joke!" she snapped. "I hope you die laughing!"

"Come on. Be a sport. After what we've been together? How we planned it all out, while intimately in bed
that evening. How you suggested it all. How I figured the
best way to write it. Well, you don't use me. Lady. Nobody
does. And nobody dumps me!"

"Oh, dear Vickie-boy. You dumped me right into
Pete's arms!"

"That was different. Just part of the plan. Get you
close to the big action, so you could be pushed the rest of the
way when things happened!"

"Things happened, all right!" she snapped, disgust-
edly.

"Well, it was easy enough to dump that light on her!
In the confusion it was easy to disappear. Nobody ever
guessed I was there! You owe me, baby! And I mean to collect in full! Pete was one thing. But...van Horn?"

"Well the ol' man, as you call him, is part of the
game, too! The real big game. The big picture! See? Just another hoop in the ladder of success!"

"You little bitch! You'd be nowhere without my
help!"

"Why you silly ass!" she savagely shrilled in a high
pitched voice. "I was on my way to the top. Now its all finished—and all because of you! You and that damn last...*joke*
of a letter!"

"It was your idea to write threatening letters to the
Palmer woman..."

"I'm not talking about that and you know it!"

"Come off it! You wouldn't be anything without
me." He now sounded desperate, eyes focused more on the
gun aimed at his gut than anything else.

She retorted, contempt and fury in her voice: "I'm

finished with you—because of you I'm finished, period! *They* found out!"

"Look," Bolton started to say. "I can fix thing…"

"Cut it!" she screamed. Tightening her grip on the gun.

"What's wrong with you?"

"Nothing that putting a nice big hole in your gut won't fix, dearie. You can laugh at my little joke, then, as you lay here bleeding to death! Some joke!"

"You little Bitch!"

"Oh, you are one to talked! Why'd you write that last note? Ruining everything?"

She sounded seriously interested, momentarily distracted. He saw his chance at maybe conning her away from killing him.

"Big deal. Big Deal! Just a gag to get your attention. You were ignoring me." Then he seemed to see a glimmer of hope, and started pleading: "But you and Horn! I hated the idea of you blowing his friggin' horn! I'm crazy about you! You're the best…in and out of bed."

"So what? Why should I care? I don't need the past clogging my future. You're the past! Just like Pete was the past. *All of you!* Why bother wiggling my ass for hired help when I can have the top dog wagging his tail in full salute in my direction."

"An old man like that?" Bolton cried, disgusted.

"Look, old, young, whatever, they're all the same in the dark, honey! Even when they need the Big Blue to keep 'em going strong. All the same. Just some damn man wanting to stick it at me! I learned how to play the game to win! And I have a nice supply of Viagra for the Horn Man." She laughed at that. "Sure. Why not? I'm smart enough to know the right men, and even docs are helpless when I let them examine me! You'd be surprised how easy they submit to my smallest whim! Ol' men like Vanny are simply delicious when they have me to fling himself at. They're grateful to get it, as if they were young studs in heat. Like a little boy with a brand new toy. I know how to make him trumpet 'do it again' through his horn. He's delighted to do me. He simply laughed in delight when I plopped those pills into his hand one evening. Not insulted at all. I said I just couldn't get enough of him. You all…disgust me! Users! You men! A girl can snap her fingers and bring you right into line. We had the whole thing locked up tight—then…. Game's over, Vic. You picked the wrong lady to screw!"

"I'll kill you—you whoring little tramp."

He leaped forward, forgetting about the gun in Judy's hand. Forgetting about the deadly threat in her eyes. Then the explosion sounded in his ears. And that was the last thing he ever heard.

* * * * * * *

Denton arrived just in time to hear the gun go off. He leaped against the door. Once in the room he came to a quick stop. He couldn't believe his eyes. At first he had thought that he would see Judy lying on the floor—but instead it was Victor who lay face down, a pool of blood already beginning to soak the rug under his head.

Judy Grant was standing over him, arms at her side. The gun was on the floor next to her feet. She turned toward Denton and then ran into his arms.

"Oh, darling, you're here! You don't know how much I need you. You gotta help me. I'll do anything. We can be together again, if you want."

Denton couldn't believe what he was hearing.

"Peter, I didn't mean it…I didn't mean to—really. honestly!" she sobbed frantically. "I didn't—God help me! Oh, God, what have *I* done!"

EPILOG

The months that followed were a dizzy run through hell and back. There was the trial where Judy Grant was let off on a manslaughter charge, but also put into an institute for the mentally insane. The shock of what had taken place was too much for her. Apparently she had a history of mental problems never brought officially out in her bios and credits. Not only had her suddenly zooming career been exploded into nothing, she had ruined every careful plan that had taken months to develop and work out.

As to Connie Remington, he couldn't stop seeing her. And their relationship just kept blooming wider and wider. The screen test he arranged for her turned out to far better than he could have imagined possible. Without any effort he arranged with Van Horn to sign Connie and place her into the part which Judy had been playing. Peter made certain it was very clear that this was his lady, untouchable! And Van Horn was so pleased with Connie's work that the word went out: hands off Connie Remington! The money lost in re-shooting the scenes was made up by the free publicity which the trial gave the picture. Then finally the film was completed and a year later...

* * * * * * *

For Connie, this was the most important day in her life. There were several reasons for that. So many things had taken place during those months. Her screen test, the contract. The film. Now it was being released.

She looked across at Peter Denton. They were at the

nightcl ub he had taken her to on their first date so many months ago. The dinner was being topped with a second martini. Connie was beginning to feel hysterically happy. This was where she'd talked to the Swinging Nancy Osborne and then danced to her lovely voice—the lady who had been saved from the seedy side of the casting couch by Disney Studios.

Well, Connie was thrilled to realize: *I have my* Disney, *right here at my side.*

She smiled and Denton smiled back. "It's been quite a day hasn't it?" she murmured

He nodded. "But it's just begun."

"I just hope the movie turns out to be a hit!"

"Why shouldn't it be? All the publicity."

"At what a horrible cost!" She shivered inwardly.

"Look, Connie. You can't blame yourself for what happened. You didn't have anything to do with it!'"

"Poor Judy."

"Stop it! Judy was twisted. Her drive was abnormal. She'd been trying much too long. Then she met Victor Bolton, and when he got that contract from Van Horn to write a movie script for Alice Palmer, the two of them just planned the whole ugly thing. Crazy as it is! A shame. But the past."

Just then Bass and Gloria La Sota came walking up.

"Have room for more?" Bass asked, sitting down in one of the other two chairs.

"More the merrier!" Denton exclaimed, obviously happy to get off the subject of Alice Palmer and Judy Grant. This was a moment for celebration.

Connie looked at Gloria and smiled, still amazed at how different the woman seemed once they'd become friends. It just proved a point that one couldn't always tell about somebody at first glance. Judy had been a shocking disappointment. Gloria a pleasant surprise. She asked the woman: "How'd things go on the set today?"

"Just fine," Gloria beamed. "We're almost finished. We rap this week."

Bass patted her hand, saying: "She's doing great. I think we'll have a neat little run with that quickie."

Gloria laughed. "Quick but legit!"

204

Bass said: "You and Van Horn were made for one another. Business-wise, that is! Fast profits for quick flicks!"

Denton nodded, then added: "Well, we're all lucky. Van Horn Productions might not be a super giant, but it's a great beginning for all of us. And you have to start somewhere!"

The PR man said: "Funny how we all kinda got a career launch—well, you guys, anyway. Me. I'm still doing my thing."

"And it's quite a neat job!" Peter Denton observed.

"And I've been doing it for a number of years, too. An ol' pro!"

Gloria beamed at him, "Not so ol' and no pro, just a wonderful man and great lover!"

"Sure, she says that about all her men!" Bass laughed, but obviously delighted.

"Only those who count can believe me, so believe!" she murmured, giving Denton a knowing wink.

"Well how is the young couple?" Bass asked, leaning forward and grinning.

Denton and Connie just looked at each other, their eyes gleaming.

The waiter came with a bottle of champagne, and few moments later the four of them were raising their glasses in salute.

"To the opening of Connie's first movie—and a life long success to the two of you," Bass announced.

Connie felt a thrill of delight as the four of them drank to that toast. It wasn't too hard to forget about the past after that. It would be easier and easier as the years went by—happily married as Mrs. Peter Denton.

And as her future husband had told her, Judy and Bolton and Palmer didn't have really anything to do with her. Except, of course, that it had all made it possible to escape the searching hands and demanding passions of the casting couchers!

That game was over.

ABOUT THE AUTHOR

Charles Nuetzel was born in San Francisco in 1934, and writes:

"As long as I can remember I wanted to be a writer. It was a dream I never thought would materialize. But with the help of Forrest J Ackerman, who became my agent, I managed to finally make it into print.

"I was lucky enough not only in selling my work to publishers but also ending up packaging books for some of them, and finally becoming a 'publisher' much like those who had bought my first novels. From there it as a simple leap to editing not only a sci-fi anthology, but a line of sci-fi books for Powell Sci-Fi back in the 1960s. Throughout these active professional years I had the chance to design some covers and do graphic cover layouts for pocket books & magazines."

Much of his work in covers and graphics are a result of having had a father who was a professional commercial artist, and who did a number of covers for sci-fi magazines in the 1950s and later for pocket books—even for some of Mr. Nuetzel's books.

In retirement he has become involved in swing dancing, a long time lover of Big Band jazz. But more interestingly world travels have taken him (and his wife Brigitte) across the world, to Hawaii, Caribbean, Mexico, Kenya, Egypt, Peru, having a life-long interest in ancient civilizations. His website is full of thousands of pictures taken during these trips.

www.ingramcontent.com/pod-product-compliance
Lightning Source LLC
Chambersburg PA
CBHW020600250626
47154CB00004B/1304